A Strait Jacket for Sarah

Cal Clark

ALL THINGS
THAT MATTER
PRESS

Acknowledgments

I'm happy to acknowledge the many debts I owe for all the help I have received with this book. Foremost, two skilled authors, Jim Buford and Marian Carcache, generously mentored me. They read and commented upon the text, leading to many improvements, large and small, and also introduced me to the complex world of publishing fiction. I can't believe the time, effort, and support that they contributed to my effort to write a murder mystery. Phil and Deb Harris of All Things That Matter Press are simply wonderful people with whom to work. In addition, Jan Widell patiently answered my many questions about psychiatric hospitals and nursing. I also received encouragement, support, and important suggests from my wife, Janet Clark, and from my three daughters, Emily Federico, Ellen Clark, and Evelyn Benavides. Period books that I consulted included *Abnormal Psychology and Modern Life* by James Coleman, *Danvers State: Memoirs of a Nurse in the Asylum* by Angelina Szot and Barbara Stillwell, *Human Problems of a State Mental Hospital* by Ivan Belknap, *Mental Hospital* by Alfred Stanton and Morris Schwartz, *Psychiatric Nursing* by Katharine Steele, *Psychiatry in Nursing* by Raymond Headlee and Bonnie Wells Corey, and *The Shame of the States* by Albert Deutsch. I also surfed the web and can recommend Googling "psychiatric nurse humor" whenever you're out of sorts.

Chapter 1 ~ Catching a Sneak

Things can get crazy at mental institutions. My name is Andy Russell. I graduated from State University with a degree in Psychology. I went to graduate school there on a research assistantship from a grant to study the development of psychiatric hospitals in the Midwest. As part of this grant, I spent the summer of 1955 working at the Elm Hill Psychiatric Hospital for Women in Osloville based on an agreement between my advisor and the hospital's Director of Nursing, Miss Carol Mason. In the mornings I worked as a nurses' aide in the Violent Ward, and after lunch I worked for Miss Mason or conducted interviews as part of the research for the project. My first month at Elm Hill was quite dramatic and a little scary. Miss Mason had to unravel the mystery concerning the murder of Daniel Adams, a prominent judge, whose daughter Carrie was committed to the hospital when all the evidence seemed to point to her guilt. In the end, Miss Mason found the real murderer with the help of an informal team of "Black Angels," named for the black rubber rainwear that several wore on the stormy night when Carrie was brought to the hospital. For almost two months after the murder was solved, things were tranquil at Elm Hill, at least as tranquil as they could be in a mental hospital.

Looking back, the psychiatric hospitals in the mid-1950s would be almost unrecognizable today. First, far more patients were institutionalized. In fact, slightly over half the hospital beds in the U.S. were in psych facilities. Second, there were few real treatments for mental patients besides psychotherapy and a crude form of electroshock, as anti-psychotic drugs were just being developed. Strait jackets were common, and treatments such as packing or wrapping a patient in wet sheets and continuous baths in which patients were placed for hours at a time were as much for restraint as for treatment. Third, many patients in mental hospitals spent years in treatment. Finally, the legal rights of the mentally ill were quite limited, if not nonexistent. For example, involuntary commitments were quite common.

Elm Hill Hospital filled almost an entire block and was made of red brick that had become somewhat tarnished over the years. Instead of a squire drab square structure, however, there were a variety of indents, rounded corners, and asymmetrical steeples that readily caught the eye that made it seem rambling and even a little winsome. Then, on second thought, it also reminded me of an old English mansion where Gothic horrors awaited innocent damsels. Similarly, I didn't see bars on the windows, so the hospital building didn't look particularly frightening, although I soon learned that the insides of all the windows on the wards were covered with strong mesh grills.

The hospital was built as part of a WPA project which involved politics, as anything big usually does. Osloville had the contacts to get a good-sized WPA project but didn't need schools or a federal building. The mayor got inspired, though, by several scandals in Downsville State Hospital in the early 1930s about the abuse of women patients. The result was a women's mental hospital whose operations would be only half financed by the state, with the other half of the budget covered by patient fees. This had several implications. The fact that there would be only female patients lessened the local opposition. The funding formula provided subsidized care for families who didn't want their loved ones confined in Downsville but simultaneously limited the patients to almost entirely upper and middle-class women. Consequently, Elm Hill has a significantly larger staff than the state facilities relative to its number of patients. There are ten wards, each with between twenty and forty patients. Our nursing duties were extensive as we had to record nearly sixty items on a behavioral chart each day and take a census of our patients each half hour.

On a Tuesday in early August 1955, I took a bus into downtown Osloville to eat at a German restaurant and see *Bad Day at Black Rock*, a thriller set in the Southwest. I was slightly disappointed because I had finally worked up enough courage to ask out Rachel Weiss, a charge nurse on the Violent Ward with whom I'd shared some scary moments at the end of the murder investigation. Normally, a "black band," as we called Registered Nurses or RNs for the black stripes on their caps, would be disdainful of lowly aides. She didn't appear to be haughty, however, and I thought that our shared experience had brought us together. Initially, she had seemed a little interested but then demurred, saying that she didn't want to get involved because I'd be leaving for

College City in less than a month. That allowed me to go in the middle of the week, rather than wait for the weekend when she would be off her 3-to-11 shift.

I got back to my room in the basement of the nurses' dormitory, Brackman Hall, about 11:00 and was too keyed up to go to bed. Thus, I started to review the notes that I'd taken from several interviews that week. The highlight for memories, although not necessarily very intellectual ones, was a long disquisition by the switchboard operator Betty Hanson on the informal culture of Elm Hill. Suddenly, about 12:30, I thought I heard noises from out in the basement where nobody should have been. The atmosphere at a mental hospital, especially after the murder investigation, had made me more nervous and cautious than I normally would have been. I turned off my light, groped my way to the door, and peered out. The basement was pitch black, but I heard more creaking noises from the far side of the cellar. Then, a narrow light appeared at floor level in the corner. It clearly wasn't because an intruder had turned on a flashlight because the light was too wide.

I was momentarily mystified. It was certainly creepy, although a ghost wouldn't need artificial light. Still, I must admit that it gave me a little shiver. Then, what must have been a trapdoor rose higher as someone pushed it up from below. With a sigh of relief, I tiptoed to the light switch for the basement and waited until the person was standing up before flicking them on. I heard a shrill shriek and saw the back of a bent-over woman holding a trapdoor with her right hand and a flashlight with her left. She froze, dropped the trapdoor and the flashlight, straightened up, put both her hands up, and asked in a frightened voice, "Are you the police?"

My heart leapt. She certainly was acting in a guilty manner. I walked up behind her. She was wearing a yellow-hooded slicker and black rubber hip boots. I also noticed a gym bag at her feet, which she had presumably put down to close the trapdoor. I pulled her left arm down and grabbed it above the elbow with my right hand, just as we'd been trained to do when subduing an agitated patient. She didn't resist, but when she saw my pajama arm, she quickly realized that it wasn't a police uniform.

"Oh, my Lord. You're Andy. What are you going to do with me?"

"I'll let Miss Mason decide. Come on."

I reached down for the flashlight and led her out of the basement and around to the front of the house. I had her ring the doorbell since she had the free hand. The door was opened by a freckled girl in a blue robe. Her initial good cheer turned to fear when she saw us.

"Oh, Nora. What have you been up to now? Why are you wearing a slicker and boots? Andy, get away. If Miss Mason finds out you've been with one of our wild girls, there'll be so much trouble."

"It's not what you think. Nora's been doing something suspicious in the basement. Please, get Miss Mason quickly."

This frightened the poor nurse even more. She turned and fled back into the house. Miss Mason, who was in her late 30s with wavy brown hair and a strong face, came within a minute. She was wearing a red robe and carrying her purse. She looked sternly at Nora, asked what she had been up to, and pulled her leather-padded handcuffs from her purse.

"I can't tell you ma'am."

"Well, let's go and see. Peggy, go back to bed. You know what will happen if I hear of tittle and tattle."

"Yes ma'am. I don't want to be scrubbing out toilets on my hands and knees." She retreated and shut off the hall light.

"Okay, Nora. You act like you've done something bad. Give me your hands. I haven't used these for almost three years, but unless you can explain yourself, I'm going to treat you like an agitated patient."

Nora just looked at her feet and made no resistance to her handcuffing. When we returned to the basement, we found that the trapdoor was normally concealed by a dirty tarp which was mostly covered with junk to discourage people from going near it. Miss Mason went through Nora's purse. There was nothing out of the ordinary in it except for a small ring with two keys on it, one of which fit the trapdoor. Miss Mason asked several times what Nora had been doing, where the stairs under the trapdoor went, and why she thought that the police were capturing her. The girl stood with slumped shoulders and a bowed head. Finally, she resignedly said, "I can't tell you." Miss Mason had me wait with our prisoner while she got dressed. She returned in about five minutes and took her away, telling her that she'd be confined to the Violent Ward for the night and turned over to the police in the morning if she weren't more cooperative.

This excitement kept me up for another hour, so I had a short night. When I checked into the Violent Ward in the basement of Elm Hill at 7:00 the next morning, Mrs. Greene, the charge nurse, told me that I had a special patient in Room 5. After removing the bedpans of Jenny Sachs and Valerie Waller, I went to wake her and get her ready for the day. I looked in through the observation porthole and saw that Nora was sitting on her bed, dressed in a hospital gown and reading a small piece of paper. I abruptly opened the door and she turned away, shoving the paper down the front of her gown. I ordered her to lie back on the bed, locked her into wrist and ankle restraints for safety, flipped up her gown, and saw the paper half shoved into the right breast of her bra. I removed it and read a message in printed block letters, "IF YOU SQUEAL, YOU'LL DROWN LIKE A RAT." Again, she refused to say anything when I asked who had given it to her and what it meant. Since someone had obviously given her contraband, I got Michelle Rice, the other nurse on our shift. We searched the room thoroughly but didn't find anything. Then I left, while Miss Rice gave Nora a full strip search.

Chapter 2 ~ Escape

I took the note to Miss Mason after breakfast, my first free moment. Since we had been exposed to the problem of fingerprints on evidence during the murder investigation, we both handled the note with gloves. She looked at it with some wonderment and said that it was time to call Laura Sanders, the policewoman who had worked on the Adams murder, to arrest and interrogate Nora. I returned to the Rubber Room, the nickname for the Violent Ward which nobody dared to utter in the presence of the Nurse Manager, June Rayburn, just in time for the 9:00 census. We had to check and record the whereabouts of the patients specifically assigned to us. My other three patients were easy to find and check off, but Nora was another thing altogether. I looked for her in the dayroom and lounge, the hydrotherapy tubs, the dining area, her room, and all the corridors. By then I was getting very nervous and had Kathy Steele, another aide, check the bathrooms and showers which were empty. I also realized that I hadn't seen Mrs. Greene anywhere.

With growing trepidation, Kathy and I knocked on the door of the Nurse Manager's suite. Miss Rayburn's secretary, the kind-hearted Mary Peters, opened the door. She saw that something was wrong and immediately called Miss Rayburn, a stout short woman with curly gray hair. We told her that Nora was missing and that we couldn't find Mrs. Greene.

Instead of blaming or questioning us, she became practical and decisive. "You'll have to tell me later how Nora ended up here. Now, we must find them. Jane could be seeing a patient in her room, but I can't see how a patient like Nora could walk through a locked door. Kathy, go check all the patient rooms. If you find Mrs. Greene, bring her to me. If you find Nora where she shouldn't be, don't approach her, but have Robert put her in a strait jacket. Andy, come with me, and we'll check the storerooms. Mary, call Miss Mason. Even if Nora got out of here, she's probably still in the hospital."

We went by the medications room which was locked and empty. Another storeroom filled with hospital supplies was empty as well. This left one last storage area that I had never visited before. When Miss Rayburn opened the door and turned on the light, she gasped and ran forward. I followed her in. The room was much smaller than the adjacent storeroom, not much bigger than a ten by ten. At the back of the room, Miss Rayburn was kneeling over a figure. Its head was hooded by what looked like a white hospital gown, the torso was tightly bundled up in a strait jacket, and the feet were tethered. Miss Rayburn turned to me with strong emotion on her face.

"Poor Jane. She's all right, thank heaven. Please, Andy, you must leave. We can't humiliate her even more. Have Mary call Miss Mason again and tell her to come to my office immediately. Then find Michelle and tell her to get all the patients into their rooms as quickly as possible. Tell them that Mrs. Green got sick suddenly and that we couldn't find another charge nurse. We'll serve them lunch there. Then come back to my office. I think Miss Mason will want you there."

When I'd run both of these errands, I returned to the Nurse Manager's office where Mary seated me at the conference table in the outer room. A few minutes later, Miss Mason appeared with Laura, the policewoman. Laura squeezed my shoulder as she sat down next to me and whispered, "You seem to be getting pulled into police work again." Mary then poured us coffee which we sipped in silence for a few minutes until Miss Rayburn brought in a shaken looking Mrs. Greene who was dressed in a hospital gown. Mary then poured them coffee and brought a plate of apple Danish from Miss Rayburn's office. Miss Mason quickly explained why she had confined Nora to the Violent Ward. Miss Rayburn then asked me to describe how I had treated her in the morning. She seemed horrified when I told the group about the note, immediately recognizing that someone who worked on either the night or morning shift must have given it to her. Laura asked if anyone had any idea what Nora had been up to, but everybody shook their heads no. Finally, Mrs. Greene, who looked much less composed than normal, got to tell her story.

Running her fingers through her unruly dark hair, she said, "During breakfast, I stayed at the nurses' station reading the notes from yesterday's shifts. Nora, who must have skipped breakfast, came up and asked for a sedative because she was so distraught that she hadn't been able to sleep all night. She also asked to be diapered because she was very nervous and had never been sedated before. After I got the diapering supplies from the nurses' station, she went with me back to the medicine room. Unfortunately, I had my purse hanging from my shoulder when she approached so she was able to steal that, too. I didn't think of it at the time, but as soon as we left the nurses' station, we were isolated and alone. I went into the medicine room and, out of the corner of my eye, I saw Nora grab something from a shelf by the door. Then, she grabbed my left arm and put a scalpel against my throat. I was so shocked and frightened that I capitulated immediately. She made me take her to the small storeroom. I doubt that she's been on this ward, so I don't know how she knew where it was or what we keep there. Once we were inside with the door closed and locked, she made me take a rubber gag off the high shelf. Then she forced me to kneel and gagged me. Next, she made me take off my uniform, slip, rubber girdle, panties, stockings, and shoes. She used her hospital gown to hood me. After that I could hear her getting restraints from the shelves. First, she diapered me standing up. She works on the Dementia Ward, so she must have a lot of experience with diapers. Second, she got me into the strait jacket. Finally, she helped me lie down on my back, put my feet around the bottom of the shelves, and buckled leg straps on me. There was a rustling of clothes for the next minute or so, as she presumably put on what she'd made me take off. Finally, she turned off the light and left. That was it until Miss Rayburn rescued me. It must have only been twenty or thirty minutes, but it felt like hours."

Miss Rayburn quickly added, "Since that storeroom is next to the side entrance into the ward, she could have easily got out unseen with Mrs. Greene's keys and been in a deserted part of the basement. Even after we alerted people to be on the lookout for a patient, someone in a nurse's uniform probably could have moved around freely."

Miss Mason was a little more reassuring. "I called the guard at the main gate. He knows Nora and is pretty sure that he hadn't seen her this morning. There are a couple of small gates through the wall, but you need special keys for them. Jane, did you have either of those keys?"

"No ma'am. Or at least I'm pretty certain I didn't. I have so many keys for the ward that there might be an odd one in the bunch, but I've never even thought of using one of those little gates."

"Also, what was in your bag? Was there anything important?"

"Well, she got my keys for everything in the ward. Other than that, the only thing that could help her was about $15 in cash and change.

"June, what are you doing with the patients now?"

"I've had them confined to their rooms. We don't have enough people to supervise them and several would probably have become upset if they had realized what was happening. We'll return to normal when the next shift comes on."

"That's good thinking. I'll have Gwen take Jane home and contact her husband.

"June, we've got a big problem with the staff, however. Someone on this shift or the preceding one must have given Nora that note and brought in the scalpel. I know you wouldn't tolerate anything dangerous like that on your ward."

Miss Mason turned her attention to the policewoman.

"Laura, what should we be doing? This brutal attack is surely criminal."

"Yes ma'am. It's aggravated assault. I'm sure we could get other major charges as well, perhaps even kidnapping. We need to get Detective Perkins here to start a full-scale investigation of the attack and her escape. Let me call police headquarters to report it and get a search started."

Chapter 3 ~ Subterranean Shenanigans

Laura then turned practical. "I'd like to investigate the passage into the basement. She obviously was up to something bad and something that must involve other people at the hospital. The horse is obviously long out of the barn, but perhaps we can find what it was chewing on. In any event, I don't think one more person would be much help in searching the hospital."

"We'll get Director Rydberg to organize the search here and talk with the police about what they want to do. Andy, you go with Laura since you know where she came up. Also, I'll get Clem to accompany you since he knows so much about the hospital and worked on its construction. Maybe, he even knows something about the tunnels. The larger key fits the trapdoor in Brackman's cellar.

"You'll need rubber coats, gloves, hip boots, and rain helmets. Nora's slicker was covered with some foul-smelling drippings, and there was muck on her boots up to her calves. Andy, it might be a good idea to get bathing caps out of our supplies here as well. I'll call Clem and have him meet you in Room 323 where the attendants keep their protective clothing."

"Thanks, Miss Mason. I don't think that I'd like to get my police rainwear smelly. Really, I don't know what I'd do if they got such foul stuff in my hair. Also, could you gather all the staff from the morning and night shifts for Richard when he gets here?"

When we stopped to get three white bathing caps, she asked why we kept such a stock of them.

"Well, it's not one of our most pleasant duties, but some of our most disturbed patients like to throw their food trays or even their bedpans at the people who are taking care of them. As I've found out, a rubber cap definitely has its uses."

"Well, that's an advantage I have. None of my prisoners have done that to me. Maybe, it's because policewomen have to always keep them in handcuffs or chains."

We met Clem on the third floor. He was a tall Negro who served as the hospital's Chief Attendant. As always, he was cheery.

"Hi, Andy. I see that your friend has had to come back to Elm Hill again. Officer, you're more beautiful than I remember. Too bad for Andy that you're wearing an engagement ring." Laura blushed and smiled.

We decided to wait to put on our protective wear until we got to the basement of Brackman. Walking around in heavy rubber clothing on a summer's day was not an appealing situation. Clem grabbed flashlights for each of us and said that he had put fresh batteries in them while he waited for us to walk up from the Violent Ward in the basement.

Once we had donned our rainwear, or, as Clem put it, "tunnel wear," Laura unlocked the trapdoor. Clem went down the steep steps first saying that he could catch us if we stumbled. After going down what seemed like the equivalent of several floors, we came out in a tunnel about six feet wide that was high enough for Clem, who's over six feet. The sides and the ceiling were brick and the floor was dirt that was topped by an inch or so of squishy mud. A few plinks on my outerwear showed the need for it. I also shined my flashlight on my gloves, which showed that they were already covered with glop from holding on to the stair railing.

Clem asked us where we thought we were, but neither of us had any idea.

"Well, I'd guess that this was built during Prohibition to bring liquor up from the river. The Muskrat provides access to Canada, you know. Old Man Brackman ran a department store. He seemed to stay prosperous when the Depression first hit, even though his store lost most of its business. Then, soon after Prohibition ended, he sold his store and house and moved away. That would suggest that he was in the liquor trade in the 1920s. If the tunnel goes to the river, however, it's going to have to drop a good deal more."

Our three flashlights provided plenty of illumination. When we shined them ahead into the distance, we saw red and yellow dots and heard a light pattering of rodent feet. The tunnel did slope downward. The sides were dirty and damp and cobwebs were everywhere. Laura patted her rubber helmet twice for reassurance and joked that she felt like Nancy Drew starting on an adventure. After what seemed at least a quarter of a mile, but probably was no more than a hundred yards, we came to a split. The bricked portion went downward in another set of stairs while a side tunnel with wooden sides and ceiling slanted off to the left. Clem guessed that this might be a link to the hospital that was added when Elm Hill was built. A short walk proved him to be correct. The tunnel ended in stairs that seemed noticeably longer than the ones we had originally descended. At the top of the stairs, there was a metal door which Laura was able to unlock. We emerged in a large closet that had three new-looking wooden boxes on its floor. Laura pulled the top off the nearest box, reached down, and started to lift a magazine from it. When she saw the cover, she gasped, then blushed, and quickly dropped the magazine back into the box.

"Oh, I didn't know that a woman could do that to men. Andy, don't look. You'll get ideas about how to attract that big hussy."

"Oh Laura, be serious. She hardly talks to me now. She told me that she likes older men."

This exchange made Clem laugh so hard he could hardly stand up. Finally, he stopped and turned serious.

"It looks like they're trying to plant contraband in the hospital again. Perhaps they never knew that we caught their last attempt in June. Well, let's see where we are."

When he opened the outer door of the closet, we found ourselves in an unused, dirty part of Elm Hill's basement. Near the closet door there was a bundled up nurse's uniform and a pair of white nurses' shoes. This time it was Laura who saw the humor in the situation.

"Someone must have been waiting for her with a new set of clothing unless, of course, Nora thought that prancing around in her lingerie would make her look inconspicuous."

There also were muddy boot tracks going to and from the closet, suggesting that Nora had been helped in her escape by someone who had come up through the tunnel. The tracks were small, leading Laura to speculate that they might belong to a woman. We then decided that exploring the tunnel would be more valuable than following muddy footsteps through the basement, and Clem led us back, starting out with an infectious chuckle.

"Well, Laura, it looks like your perm needs as much protection in some parts of the hospital as in the tunnel."

"I like your humor, Clem, but I still have a pretty queasy feeling. We had a horrible murder here three months ago. Who knows what's going on now. About the only good thing about this is that this gives me another chance to work with Matt and Richard again because of the female suspect and witnesses. My normal lieutenant really doesn't seem to know what to do with a policewoman, so this is a treat in several ways."

This piqued my curiosity. "What do policewomen do in Osloville, Laura?"

"There are three of us assigned to each shift. The male officers who take calls can request us to help them when there are family disturbances or female prisoners or witnesses. On my shift, the lieutenant discourages this unless a woman has been arrested. I get the impression that he thinks that Bridget Devlin and I are cute, so he finds lots of excuses to call us into his office. Still, he was happy when Richard requested that I be assigned to his team during the Adams murder."

Clem brought us back to Nora's escape. "Well, let's hope we find something more. This would be an easy way out for her, but somebody must have given her a key, too, since we have the one she used last night. It looks like we better see where those stairs go. While I wouldn't want to go walking around here in my good shoes, we've certainly haven't found anything requiring hip boots yet. Coming out in Brackman's basement wouldn't do her that much good today. Laura, could you please lock the door behind us? There's no point in leaving a way for anybody else to go wandering."

It took three sets of stairs and two short corridors before we came to a rusty door with the sound of running water on the other side. We were clearly close to the river as the evidence of vermin became much more noticeable and bothersome. The drip of nasty slime on us also got worse as we descended. After Laura opened the door, we came out in a small room with metal walls, a plank ceiling, and a very muddy floor. Laura was the first to spot the new clues.

"Oh, look! There're boot tracks in the mud."

She squatted on the edge of the wooden platform and shined her light on the floor of the room that was about eight inches below.

"Several of them have rugged bottoms like the boots we're wearing, but there's one set that's off to the side a little which seems dressier."

Clem bent over the footprints. "That looks like the pattern on the knee boots that the nurses wear. Also, there's a blob on the left heel of the boots. That should make her boot easy to recognize if we ever find it."

At Laura's direction, we then stepped off the platform at its far end and stayed well away from all the other tracks as we crossed the room. At the far side, Laura opened another rusty door, leading us to a large concrete bowl that took up most of the area in a cave that extended fifty feet behind the cliff face. A second glance showed that the bowl was part of a sewerage system that was odiferous. Large pipes that you could walk through entered and exited the cave parallel to the river, and there was another pipe from the ceiling, presumably for Elm Hill's wastes. At one time this basin had been routed into the river through an opening which was about six feet high and which narrowed from five feet across at the bottom to two feet at the top. This entrance to the cave was covered by a heavy metal grate that was old and heavily rusted, just like the two doors that we'd come through. The old spillway was now blocked by a four-foot high concrete barrier that evidently was enough to protect the river from the sewerage flowing through the basin.

Clem raised his flashlight toward the entrance. The grate was secured by a padlocked latch on the opposite side of the spillway from where we were standing.

Laura said, "Oh, Lord. I can see why we needed all this protective wear. I certainly wouldn't have wanted this evil stuff on my uniform boots. Clem, would you mind examining this room while Andy and I go outside and see if we can find where they went to? Don't go into those awful pipes, however."

"That's fine but let me make a suggestion. Let Andy hold your hand or arm because you seem to be stumbling in your hip boots."

Laura evidently saw the wisdom in this because she grabbed my hand firmly and whispered.

"Keep a firm grip. I don't know how I'd ever get clean again if I fell in this awful mess."

Wading through the knee-deep sewerage was a little tricky, but we made it to the grate with no mishaps. When we got to the opening, we noticed a raised rotting wooden platform just beyond it which was covered with four or five pairs of hooded raincoats and gloves but no boots. Most had been used recently since they were damp and smelly. Laura bent over them and gagged, so I offered to go through the pockets of the raincoats. Only one raincoat had anything in it. I pulled a half-empty packet of cigarettes and some matches from The Robbers' Roost out of the pocket of the third slicker.

Laura sounded far heartier than I would have expected given the oppressive cavern and said, "Good work, Andy, The Robbers' Roost is the main hangout of the Griggs gang. Nora has obviously got herself into some bad company."

Once Laura got the gate unlocked, I gave her another caution. "I get the feeling that you've never been in hip boots before."

"Well, I guess that's obvious. My brothers wanted to take me fishing with them, but it never appealed to me."

"There may be rocks in the riverbed, so put each foot down very carefully or you might fall. The river is much cleaner than the sewerage pipe, but a tumble would be unpleasant."

She took that seriously as we waded slowly through the Muskrat. We started off downstream but stopped when we could see a string of houses with lawns coming down to the river bank. We decided that this layout would be too conspicuous for people in rubber rainwear wading with no apparent purpose. We then turned back and slowly sloshed for almost a quarter of a mile to where small stream entered the Muskrat. There were several boot prints in the mud by the stream, but Laura decided that we had gone far enough.

Clem said that he hadn't found anything suspicious and interpreted what we had seen in the tunnels. "In the bad old days before Osloville built a sewerage treatment plant with WPA funds, the sewerage from the top and sides of Elm Hill was piped into the cave so it could empty into the river. I'd guess that the rum runners probably took advantage of this when they built the tunnels we're in. They could lock the outlet from the cave, and nobody was likely to try to break in because of the sewerage. The hospital and the wastewater treatment plant were built at the same time. I hadn't thought of it before, but the hospital's sewerage would probably have overwhelmed the cave and its spillway. Finally, I'd guess that someone found the old tunnel when they were working on the new sewerage system and built the connection to the hospital basement."

Chapter 4 ~ Questioning

After our return from exploring the tunnels, we split up. Laura went into the administrative suite in search of Detective Perkins. Clem said that he'd go see if several attendants could be spared from other wards to help monitor the Violent Ward for the rest of the day shift. For my part, I descended to the Violent Ward in the basement where a very nasty surprise awaited me. As I was walking up to the nurses' station, an older nurse whom I didn't know, pointed to her left to indicate the door into the Nurse Manager's office suite. When I looked in I saw a stern-looking policewoman in her mid-30s sitting at the secretary's desk and talking on the telephone. She pointed to my left to the conference room and continued her conversation. Another policewoman, young with nice black hair and a cute face, must have seen me because she emerged from the conference room. Her tone was quite official, however.

"Hello. You must be Andy Russell. I'm officer Devlin. Because you're being questioned in a criminal investigation, you must be searched. Also, I have to secure you when you're under escort. As I understand it, you've been in Officer Sanders' custody. Is that true?"

"I've been with her for the last hour or so. We just parted when we got back to the hospital a couple of minutes ago."

"She should have escorted you back down here, but I guess it's okay. Don't tell Officer Riston or there'll be trouble. Here, give me your right hand."

She detached a handcuff from her belt and locked it on my right wrist while keeping a firm grip on the unlocked cuff. She then pulled me into the conference room. All the members of my shift were there, as well as two women attendants from the night shift. All of them looked either glum or angry, probably because they had one wrist cuffed to their chairs. Officer Devlin handed me a patient's gown from a chair by the door and picked up a pair of black rubber gloves.

"Don't worry, Andy. I'm sure you'll be released after your interrogation. I'm sorry about the handcuffs, but we're required to use them when we escort someone, especially a male. If I hadn't specifically asked the detectives about it, I'm sure Officer Riston would have ordered body probes. I guess that it's just hard to be nice to someone in custody."

As we were coming up to the nurses' station on our way back from the staff restrooms where I had had my strip search, Officer Devlin had a word of advice.

"Officer Hastings will take you up for your interrogation. You need to be submissive. She's not mean like Officer Riston, but she keeps her prisoners under strict control and won't tolerate any backtalk."

Once we were back in the Nurse Manager's suite, Officer Devlin handed me over to a tall blond policewoman who had a pretty but stern face. She quickly cuffed my hands behind my back, used another set of handcuffs to attach my cuffs to her wrist, and grabbed my right arm with a surprisingly strong grip.

"Thank you, Bridget. Mr. Russell, I'm Officer Nell Hastings. I'm taking you upstairs and expect your complete cooperation. Do you understand?"

She was even more intimidating than I expected.

"Yes, ma'am. I understand. I have to handle restrained patients almost every day."

When we got to the conference room, she escorted me to the chair at the head of the table, unlocked my handcuffs, and sat me down. Then she took the seat on my left and re-cuffed my wrist to the arm of my chair. This seemed to amuse Detective Perkins.

"Hello, Andy. Nell and the girls seem to have made you a little nervous. Let's hope that they can get under the skin of someone who's got a guiltier conscience than I'm sure yours is."

Besides Officer Hastings, Detective Perkins partner, Matt Kempton, Laura's fiancé who seemed to enjoy my discomfort, was also present. I started by telling them about catching Nora in the basement and about what I had seen earlier in the morning on the Violent Ward. They had presumably heard most, if not all of it, from Miss Mason. Thus, there were no follow-up questions on these matters. Instead, Detective Perkins moved on to the broader question about who could have got the contraband to Nora.

"How do you think that her confederates learned that Nora was in trouble, Andy?"

"There several ways. Most obviously, somebody on the night shift could have seen Miss Mason dragging her in. Or, somebody at Brackman overheard us. Everyone has their windows open now. In particular, quite a few people from the 3 to 11 shift would still be awake. Perhaps, Nora was supposed to call someone when she got home safely. The problem with all these possibilities, however, is that they would involve calling out through the hospital switchboard, which would make it dangerous to have a suspicious conversation because, especially at night, the operators do a lot of eavesdropping. Have you checked with the night shift operator?"

"There were no calls to or from the Violent Ward after midnight. There were at least a few calls out of Brackman, but if any of them were suspicious the operators didn't pick up on it. We woke up the guy who had been night guard at the gate, and he said that nobody left after midnight."

"There are a couple of other possibilities for getting out of Elm Hill. First, there are the tunnels that I'm sure Laura has told you about, although I don't know how likely it was that they could have been used. The night staff on the Violent Ward would have had to have been gone so long if they went out through them that their absence would almost certainly have be noticed. They would be unable to claim that they had gone out for a smoke or a quick trip to the cafeteria to get a snack. The women in Brackman wouldn't have had to worry about the time, but I was so keyed up last night that it would have been hard for somebody to go stumbling around the basement in the dark without being discovered.

"There's another possibility, however. When she was interviewing Mrs. Greene this morning, Miss Mason mentioned the two small side gates to the hospital grounds. I got the impression that the number of keys is pretty limited, but if someone had one, they could get out without being seen."

"Well, Andy. That's a great idea that we hadn't thought of. Nell, could you please call downtown and have them check with the two taxi companies to see whether they picked up anyone near Elm Hill early this morning? They shouldn't get much business from around here at that time. Once you're done with that, it's probably time for Laura to get our new suspect."

We had a short and silent break while Officer Hastings left. Then, Detective Perkins resumed his questioning.

"Tell me, Andy. How difficult would it be for someone on your shift or the night shift to get the contraband to Nora?"

"Obviously, that's something I've thought about. If they had the tunnel keys and the scalpel, it would be much easier for someone on the night shift than on ours to plant them in the medicine room and to leave the note in her room. There are only four on that shift, as opposed to seven on ours. In addition, all the patients are locked up, so I'm sure that there are extended times when the staff don't move around very much. On the other hand, a big question would be how someone on the night shift could have gotten the keys and scalpel since they must have come from outside the ward. In contrast, anyone on our shift could have brought things in, but getting access to Nora and the storage rooms would be much chancier."

"That's what Miss Mason said. So, could you go over the opportunity that people on the day shift had. Let's start with what would be the time frame."

"Because of the seriousness of it, I checked my watch once I confiscated the note from Nora. It said 7:47. So, whoever did it must have been out of her cell at least three or four minutes earlier. I didn't see anyone in the corridor, although they could've gone into another room to attend a patient or into one of the staff washrooms that are at the front of that corridor. The time frame would be from when people arrived on the ward to 7:45 at the latest. In addition, Mrs. Greene, the charge nurse, has a brief meeting at the start of each shift. That's where she told me that I should take care of Nora, for example. I didn't check my watch, but I'd guess that it went approximately from 7:05 to 7:15."

"When do people arrive? Do they clock in?"

"People try to be there a few minutes before seven. Mrs. Greene comes a little earlier because she has to consult with the charge nurse from the night shift. We don't have to punch a card to go on or off duty. At least from what I've seen our staff is pretty responsible."

Detective Perkins then tried to hone in on who was where.

"Who's on your shift, Andy?

"Our supervisor or charge nurse is Jane Greene, and the other nurse who works with us is Michelle Rice. There are two attendants, Robert Martindale and Bertha Bartholomew, a nursing student, Helga Gerlach, and two aides, Kathy Steele and myself. The Nurse Manager and her secretary work from 9 to 5, so they didn't come on duty until well after the critical period."

"What can you tell me about your and other people's movements?"

"Unfortunately, detective, I can't be that helpful. I was the last person into the ward when I got there a few minutes before seven. As I was approaching the hospital, I saw Robert and Helga about thirty yards ahead of me. The three of us, therefore, couldn't have done anything before Mrs. Greene's meeting. After the meeting, Mrs. Greene talked to me for three or four minutes, telling me about our strange new patient and asking me what I thought 'Naughty Nora' had gotten into last night. After that, I went into the dining room to grab two donuts and started my rounds to wake up the four patients specifically assigned to me a little early. The first two were in the two corridors between the nurses' station and the main entrance, so I was totally out of sight of Nora's room and the storeroom corridor until I went to her room. There were several other people I saw when I was caring for my first two patients. Kathy Steele was definitely there, and I do remember Helga because she's so tall. Also, Mrs. Greene was at the nurses' station when I went past it."

"Well, that should wrap things up about last night and today, Andy. I'd like you to stay for another few minutes to hear what our suspect has to say."

Officer Hastings uncuffed me from the hot seat at the head of the table, sat me down in the next chair, and after a brief hesitation reattached the cuff to her own wrist.

Chapter 5 ~ An Arrest

Detective Perkins then called out to Laura. She quickly brought in an extremely frightened Rachel Weiss. Rachel had been fully shackled. Her wrists were secured to a chain that was tightly locked around her waist, a chain down her front connected her waist and leg chains, and another chain ran from her back to Laura's belt. Laura sat at the head of the table maintaining a strong grip on the prisoner's arm. Detective Perkins started his interrogation in a surprisingly gentle tone.

"Miss Weiss. Do you know why you're here and in shackles?"

"No, sir. I really don't. The policewoman told me that something very bad happened in the Violent Ward and that someone had raised suspicions about me. Then she made me go out of our room when she searched it. After that, she took me into custody. I don't have any idea about what this could be about. Please, sir. I haven't done anything bad."

"Do you know Nora Thomas?"

"Yes, of course I do. She's a nurse on Ward 2. We both live in Brackman, but I don't know her very well. She's pretty wild, and I'm quite shy."

"Well, Nora was caught acting very suspiciously late last night. When she refused to explain herself, Miss Mason locked her in the Violent Ward for the night and told her that she'd be turned over to the police if she didn't confess in the morning. Before Miss Mason could see her this morning, however, she assaulted the charge nurse and escaped. Do you know anything about it?"

"Oh, Lord. That's horrible. Poor Mrs. Greene. Please believe me, I wasn't involved. How could I have been?"

"Well, later investigation found that Nora had been involved in smuggling in contraband last night through tunnels that go up from the Muskrat to the hospital and your dormitory. She escaped through the tunnels this morning after subduing Mrs. Greene with a scalpel. What do you know about that?"

"Please, sir. I don't know anything about it."

"Well, the guard at the front door of the hospital says that you didn't go back to Brackman until almost 2:00, although your shift ended at

11:00. What were you doing? Think before you answer. If you try to lie, Officer Sanders will take you straight to the Osloville Jail. Do you understand?"

"Yes, sir. Please, I have no reason to lie. We got a catatonic schizophrenic who was admitted to Elm Hill at the beginning of the week. I've had hardly any experience with patients with that diagnosis, so I went to our medical library to try to get a better understanding of her condition and what Dr. Sessions, her psychiatrist, is trying to do."

"Aren't you just supposed to follow his orders? When we get an order from a superior officer, we better obey and not ask questions. Do you like to argue with doctors?"

"No, sir. Of course not, but the more I understand about what the doctor is trying to do, the better I can help the patient."

"Well, let's move on. We've been told that this isn't the first time you've been caught acting suspiciously. Do you know what I mean?"

"No, sir. Please, sir. Really, I don't."

I noticed that poor Rachel was sounding more and more frightened, so I reached over to her with my free hand. When she felt my hand, she grabbed it and squeezed it hard.

"Well, let me remind you then. On the night that the Adams murder investigation came to a head, didn't Andy here catch you planting pornography and drugs? Then, didn't you seduce him to throw him off the track and try to wheedle information about Miss Mason out of him?"

"That's not true! Why do you think such horrible things?"

"Do you deny that he caught you hiding pornography? Or that you left your underwear in the cell? Look, he's holding your hand now."

Rachel began to sob. I silently cursed Molly Wells who almost certainly was the source of this greatly distorted gossip and decided that I could answer better for Rachel than she probably could at this point.

Stifling my own anger, I interjected in a calm voice. "Don't you remember, Detective Perkins, that you heard a tape in which April Gibbs claimed that she and Amy Strong were the ones who had distributed the contraband? There doesn't seem to be any reason to suspect Miss Weiss. What actually happened was that when I checked the room, I saw that she was pulling the magazine out from under the mattress. What she said when Miss Mason questioned her later was that she had found the magazine when she inspected the room during her shift. At first, she intended to tell Mrs. Rayburn about it when she came back on duty the following Monday. But then as she was leaving the hospital, she changed her mind and thought that she should take it to her nurse manager since they both live in Brackman Hall.

"I'm sure Rachel is too embarrassed to tell you the rest. You had just told us about the plot to plant drugs and pornography to create a scandal and help some unscrupulous men take over Elm Hill. Thus, when I saw the magazine, I thought that she was trying to get Miss Mason arrested and disgraced. I admit that I was very angry with her. I put her in bed restraints and went to call Miss Mason. When I got back to the room, she said that she knew she had to be restrained and asked if she could be diapered. That's why Thomas and April found her panties in the room. We most certainly didn't have sex. I thought she was wicked at the time. I'm holding her hand now because she's humiliated and frightened. She isn't trying to seduce me, either. In fact, she just turned down a date with me.

"Finally, when Miss Mason was questioning her that night, she went over her nurse's notes. She was very impressed with how sophisticated they were and with her ability to understand what the psychiatrists were trying to do. Her going to the medical library sounds much more credible than it would for most other nurses."

Laura replied in a kindly tone but didn't seem willing to concede Rachel's innocence.

"From what you know, Andy, that makes sense, but I hope that you don't think that I would have chained her up because of some speculative gossip. She's under arrest because of what we've found in her room.

"Now, Rachel. Does the hospital supply you with a set of rainwear?"

"Yes, ma'am. We have rubber raincoats, helmets, and boots."

"Can you identify yours?"

"Yes, ma'am. Because there're so many, I put a piece of white tape with my name on it inside each item."

"Where are they now?"

"They're in a closet in our room. Both my roommate Shelley and I have separate closets for our normal clothes, and we also share a third closet for our outerwear."

"When was the last time you wore them?"

"We had a stormy day a week before last Thursday, so I wore the full set of rainwear when I walked back and forth between my dormitory and the hospital."

"Did you walk through mud? Are your boots muddy now?"

"Oh no, ma'am. I just walked on the pavement and sidewalk. In any event, I would have wiped any mud off my boots when I got back to Brackman. I'm tidy."

"What about gum on the bottom of a boot?"

"Oh, I'd definitely scrape that off. I think that's yucky."

"Rachel, how could you think you could get away with such lies? Your boots have smelly mud on them that goes well above the ankles. In addition, there's a glob of gum on the left heel. There were several prints from a nurses' boot like that in the tunnels. I'll go back down there to match your boot with the prints when we're done here. Unless they don't match, you'll be arrested for complicity with Nora and her crimes."

Rachel squeezed my hand harder and started to cry in earnest. Detective Kempton, who likes to play bad cop a little too much for my taste, added another nasty perspective to the interrogation.

"Rachel, you're obviously not married, and you didn't want to go out with Andy. I'm starting to wonder how shy you really are. Have you been in bed with another crooked doctor, like the female aides and attendants we arrested in June?"

Rachel stopped crying and turned first to Laura and then to me.

"Please, Officer Sanders, I'm not a slut. Could you have Miss Mason examine me? You'd take her word, wouldn't you? Thank you, Andy, for sticking up for me. You can't know how much it means to me. Please believe me, I'm innocent."

Laura looked to Detective Perkins. "What do you want me to do, sir?"

"That's probably a good idea. Could you please see if Miss Mason is available before lunch? Also, take Andy along and see how much of his story she can confirm, but he certainly doesn't need to be handcuffed."

"Certainly, sir."

As Officer Hastings unsnapped the cuffs that linked us, Laura got Rachel up on her feet and admonished us. "If people see you two holding hands, there'll be even more nasty gossip." She then led us around the administrative suite to the office of Mrs. Holdstrom, Miss Mason's secretary, who told us that she was free.

Unlike Mrs. Holdstrom, who had had to stifle a giggle when she saw how Laura had restrained Rachel, Miss Mason looked a little grim as she had Laura sit us around her small conference table.

"Hello, Laura. I've been told that you and the other policewomen have been pretty liberal with your handcuffs, but why are you bringing poor Rachel to me chained up like a condemned murderess?"

Laura blushed. "Please ma'am. Since we're not in a secure police station, Officer Riston made us be very strict. I know you use restraints on dangerous patients. Here, we don't know who might be dangerous until they're fully interrogated, but Rachel has been shackled because she's been put under arrest."

Since I figured that Miss Mason had probably been eavesdropping on the detectives through an intercom, I wondered if she were trying to put Laura at a disadvantage. It didn't seem to intimidate her, however, as she outlined what Rachel and I had said.

"Well, Laura, I'm happy to confirm everything that they said about the past except Andy's asking her out, about which I simply don't know. I don't know anything about last night and her boots, of course, but I think that the accusation that she was helping Nora because she's having an affair with an unsavory doctor sounds almost off the wall. We can take Miss Weiss to the exam room in the Admissions Department. It should be free."

They returned in about ten minutes. Miss Mason smiled and told me that Detective Kempton's suspicions had turned out to be baseless. She then turned solicitous for the police detail. "Well, I see that it's already getting close to noon. Gwen can have the cafeteria workers bring up lunches to the conference room for Detectives Perkins and Kempton. What about you? Also, how many should I have sent to the Violent Ward in addition to the ones for the patients?"

"I'll eat here as well. I'll call the jail and get the matron's aide to come get Rachel since all the policewomen on our shift are busy here. I think that there are eight people who need lunches in the Violent Ward. There are three policewomen and the five staff members for the day shift, excepting Mrs. Greene and Andy. The secretary, is free to go to lunch, of course, since she doesn't have to be interrogated."

Miss Mason and Laura left for a moment to give their instructions to Mrs. Holdstrom, leaving Rachel chained to a chair.

"Oh, Rachel. I'm so sorry for you."

"Thank you so much, Andy. I'm really scared, but I know that I'm innocent."

"How did the policewoman treat you? Was she mean?"

"No, she was professional, but she scared me when she took me into custody and told me that I better tell the truth. Once she got me to the Violent Ward for my body search, she became more sympathetic, perhaps because I was beginning to cry. Actually, she seemed a little hesitant once she pulled her rubber gloves on, so I told her how we were taught do an exam. Did she do you?"

"No, Officer Devlin searched me but didn't do a body probe."

Just then, Miss Mason and Laura returned. Once Laura had taken poor Rachel away, Miss Mason told me that I didn't need to finish my shift and that I should come back to her office at 2:00.

Chapter 6 ~ A Trudge in the Mud

I found Officer Hastings waiting for me outside Miss Mason's office. For a moment, I thought that she was there to arrest me, but she kept her handcuffs in her purse.

"Mr. Russell. You're to show me the tunnels and then we'll try to follow the tracks that Officer Sanders found. I've done a lot of hunting and fishing and am good at tracking. You certainly don't have to worry about me wobbling in my hip boots.

"Also, I have a bone to pick with you. You called Officer Sanders 'Laura.' You need to be more respectful of authority. Still, you were a good boy when you were in my custody."

"Yes, ma'am."

We walked silently together to the basement of Brackman where we had left our still odiferous protective garments. Once we were there, Officer Hastings pulled two bathing caps from her purse, tossed one to me, and gave me instructions in a kinder voice than she had used before.

"Officer Sanders said that we shouldn't put the old caps directly on our heads because they're stinky. We'll double cap with these on the bottom. Here's a medical mask and goggles to protect you face."

Once we were dressed, she examined me to make sure that everything was where it should be, even pulling the chinstrap of my bottom bathing cap tighter. She must have noted my surprise.

"Mr. Russell, you're not my prisoner now, but I still feel responsible for you. Now, stay about ten feet behind me in the tunnels so that the tracks don't get even more messed up."

Once we got to the first tunnel, she confirmed that there was only one set of footprints going toward Brackman. Then, she literally threw up her hands sending slime flying from her rubber gloves when we reached the turnoff to Elm Hill. Unhappily, she said that the floor was such a mess that trying to discern anything was hopeless. She had me walk beside her and took a firm grip of my left arm.

"You may not as be ungainly as Officer Sanders in hip boots, but you haven't been as sure-footed as I'd like. Now, hold tight to the railing. These steps are really slippery after they've been tracked up so much."

She was right that I felt more insecure than the first time through the tunnels. She caught me when I slipped slightly on some mud in a lower passageway and again when I stumbled over a rock in the over-the-knee sludge in the waste-treatment basin. The second stumble shook me up a little.

"Thank you, ma'am. I think I would've gone down into this awful muck without your help."

"You're welcome. Officer Sanders said that you saved her twice. In any event, I don't think that you'll be arrested. After all, you're the one who captured Nora in the first place."

As soon as we left the cave, Officer Hastings had us remove our slickers, helmets, and bathing caps to "keep us from getting wetter on the inside than the outside." She also kept her firm grip on me as we sloshed up the river to where Nora and her companion had apparently left the Muskrat. Here, the officer's tracking skills were quite valuable. She confirmed that two people, including Nora's presumed companion, identifiable by the boot prints from Elm Hill's basement, had clambered up into a tiny stream She also said that both sets of tracks were probably made by women's waders.

We clambered up a steeper part of the bank to avoid disturbing the tracks of the fugitives. I went first and had to use my hands and knees, which made me glad that I was still wearing gloves and boots, and then pulled Officer Hastings up the steep seven-foot shelf. Once we both had sound footing, she got us organized.

"Okay, Mr. Russell. We'll roll our boot tops down under the knees, so we can walk more naturally. Also, I guess that we should carry our gloves with us in case we need them. Now stay on my left side at all times to keep from contaminating their trail, tell me if you see anything suspicious, and don't touch anything."

Nora and her companion had kept to the streambed which was more mud than water since it hadn't rained for almost two weeks. Consequently, their two sets of tracks were easy to follow. After about fifty yards, the stream swung to the right away from us and headed toward the hill. Officer Hastings grabbed my arm.

"Stay exactly where you are. I don't think that they wanted to climb Elm Hill again."

She moved upstream for a few steps and stopped.

"They left the stream and headed toward the park that's about half a mile to our left. I should be able to follow them without too much difficulty. I think you should walk back up the hill to the hospital. You'll still have time to shower and change clothes before you're due in Miss Mason's office.

Chapter 7 ~ Suspicious Aides

When I returned to Miss Mason's office, she was sitting pensively at her desk. She smiled when I walked in and had me tell her all about the tunnels and tracking Nora and her accomplice. When I finished, she seemed to be in a much better mood.

"Well, Andy. That's quite a surprise. If Rachel's arrest and this new attack on Elm Hill weren't so disturbing, finding the tunnels might be intriguing and romantic. We could even make up ghost stories about them."

Just then her telephone rang. "Hello. Mary? Thanks for letting me know.

"Andy, this is why I had you come back here. They're going to interview the rest of the staff on your shift now. If you listen in with me, you might pick up something."

We went to the little room behind the conference room that had a sign saying Janitor's Closet but in reality, held a small table and recording equipment for a hidden microphone somewhere in the conference room. Almost immediately, we heard the door open and Detective Perkins greet the newcomers.

"Thank you for bringing him up, Laura. Please stay."

"You're welcome, sir. Here, Robert. Please sit down. There, are you comfortable?"

"Yes, ma'am."

Then Detective Perkins started the questioning.

"Mr. Martindale, is it true that you've worked on the Violent Ward for just over a month?"

"Yes, I moved there from Ward 7."

"Have you seen anything suspicious there?"

"No, I haven't noticed anything out of the ordinary. Everyone is so busy that all I've seen is people trying to care for our patients."

"Okay. Can you describe what you did and who you saw this morning before about 7:45."

"Sure. I got there a couple of minutes before seven. Helga Gerlach, the student nurse, had walked over from Brackman with me. When we came into the ward, she went directly to the nurses' station while I detoured to the kitchen to get a cup of coffee. I then went to the nurses' station where Mrs. Greene, our charge nurse, gave us our briefing. Everyone was there by the time I came up. I checked my watch when the meeting finished, and it was a minute or two before 7:15.

"I didn't have anything to do specifically until about 7:45 when I start collecting and cleaning the bedpans that are put outside the rooms when the staff wake the patients up. So, I went to check the bathroom and shower area to make sure that the night attendants had cleaned them adequately. Sometimes they're lazy. I think that it's important that the patients start the day in a good environment. I had just entered the bathroom area when I heard a noise behind me and turned to see Helga stooping over to pick up a small bag."

"Where do you think she was going?"

"She was going away from the nurses' station, so the only places she could go were the corridor with Nora's room on it or the lounge. She was wearing her protective clothing, so it looked like she was on her way to take care of a patient."

"What do you mean by protective clothing? Why would she need it?"

"She was wearing a black rubber apron and gloves, as well as a bathing cap, and surgeon's mask. The aides have to wear them when they're taking care of patients who throw food and human waste at them."

"Did you get a good look at her? Are you absolutely sure it was Helga?"

"Because of her cap and mask, I didn't see her face. Also, because she was stooped down, I couldn't be certain that the woman was as tall as Helga. Still, it must have been her because her rubber cap was blue, like Helga's. All the others have white caps."

"What did you do then?"

"I inspected the showers and the bathroom. I found a couple of messy toilets, so I cleaned them. By then it was 7:30, so I went back to the kitchen, which was empty, to have another cup of coffee and a donut before I started my rounds. I didn't see anything out of the ordinary and didn't realize that anything was wrong until the cry went up after Nora's escape."

"Thank you for being so cooperative, Mr. Martindale."

After we heard the door open and close, Detective Perkins continued. "Laura, please call down and have Bridget bring Helga up. After what we've heard she looks suspicious, so she should be fully shackled."

Laura returned quickly, and the three bantered for several minutes until there was a sharp knock on the door. Laura evidently got up and opened it.

"Oh, thanks so much, Bridget. Did she give you any trouble?"

"No, she didn't resist, but she broke down while I was chaining her up."

Laura seemed more accommodating toward Helga than usual. "Here, let me take her. Maybe, you should stay, however, in case we have to take her into custody.

"Now, be a good girl, Helga. If you haven't done anything wrong, you won't get in trouble. I'll sit next to you if you need a tissue. I know you can't help yourself with your hands cuffed to your waist chain."

"Please, ma'am. Why did she do this to me? That's not the way the others were treated. Please, ma'am. I don't know anything about Nora."

Detective Perkins then took over the interrogation. "We've learned something very suspicious about you, Miss Gerlach. You must tell us the exact truth, or you'll get in more trouble. Do you understand?"

"Yes, sir. Please believe me. I don't have anything to hide."

"Describe what you did and who you saw from the time you got to the Violent Ward until 7:45."

"I came in a few minutes before seven with Robert Martindale, the attendant. I went straight to the nurses' station, while he went into the kitchen to get a cup of coffee. Andy was close behind me and all the other staff were already there. After the meeting, I went to the kitchen for coffee and a donut. They had chocolate-frosted ones this morning, which is rare. Bertha came in with me for coffee but left right away with her full cup. She came back a few minutes later, and we chatted until it was time to go. I left at 7:30 to wake my patients up. None of the four I'm taking care of right now are on the corridor where Nora was being held, so I can't tell you anything about that. My first three patients were on the two corridors between the main entrance and the nurses' station. I didn't check my watch, but I'm sure it was around 7:45 by the time I finished with them. I also saw Miss Rice and Andy as I went from one of these patients to another, but I really don't remember the exact circumstances since we all were so busy."

"Were you wearing protective clothing, Helga?"

"Yes, sir. I put on my rubber gloves to handle the bedpans. I don't have any messy patients since Kathy Steele took them over, so there's no need for anything else."

"Do you deny that you keep a blue bathing cap on the ward?"

"No, sir, of course not. I have to wear a swim suit and the cap when we shower the patients on Tuesday, Thursday, and Saturday."

"Who else has a cap on your shift?"

"Kathy has to use one every day because she takes care of the messy patients. Bertha regularly uses hers for the showering, and Miss Rice keeps a swim suit and rubber cap for emergencies in case she has to go into the showers. Andy had to wear a cap daily when he took care of Mrs. Strickland and Miss Peters and may still have it in his locker."

"You have a blue cap. What colors are the other ones?"

"All the ones that I've seen are white, sir."

"Well, there's a major problem, Helga. A woman in a blue cap and surgeon's mask was seen walking toward the corridor where Nora was being held at the time when you claim that you were munching donuts. Do you want to reconsider what you've told us? Telling lies will only get you in worse trouble."

"Please, sir. It wasn't me. Please believe me."

Laura interrupted. "From what you said, I wonder whether you were in the kitchen. Andy said that he went to get donuts after the staff meeting but didn't say anything about seeing anyone. Are you sure that you're telling the truth?"

Yes, ma'am. I'm telling the truth. If Andy just got donuts, they were in the dining room. The coffee was in the kitchen behind the dining room. I grabbed a donut on my way in and then chatted with Bertha in the kitchen."

Detective Perkins responded, "Well, that's certainly something we can check on. You'll need to stay in custody until we investigate further. Laura, could you please ask Miss Mason if there's a place that we can keep her here until we make a final decision about what to do with her."

Miss Mason quickly rose and headed back to her office so she'd be there when Laura arrived. Officer Devlin tried to sooth a sobbing Helga.

A few minutes later the door opened as Laura returned. "Please, sir. Miss Mason suggested locking her up in the cell where Nora was held since it's been searched by both the Elm Hill staff and us. The substitute charge nurse has a key."

"That's fine with me. Bridget, could you please take her back down and bring us Kathy Steele. Also, have the ward searched for bathing caps."

"Yes, sir. Come along, Helga. Let's hope the search helps you."

The detectives and Laura followed Officer Devlin and her prisoner out of the conference room. Miss Mason returned to our hidey-hole as they were leaving and whispered that Mrs. Holdstrom would bring us coffee and sweet rolls in a few minutes.

The two men returned first. Then Laura came in. "Bridget said to tell you that she thinks that Kathy is a hard case. All the others seem frightened or humiliated, but she was cool as a cucumber even during her personal search. Let me get her for you. I left her handcuffed to a door handle."

After Kathy was brought in and settled, Detective Perkins took over the questioning. "Miss Steele, it's very important that we trace everyone's movements up to 7:45 this morning. Do you understand?"

"Of course."

"Please tell us what you did and whom you saw."

"I got to the hospital about ten before seven. I went straight down to the ward and then went into the kitchen to get a mug of coffee. Bertha, who makes the coffee, was just leaving. I went back out and looked up the corridor to the nurses' station. I was hoping to talk to Mrs. Greene about one of my patients, but she wasn't there. So, I went back to the kitchen to finish my coffee and get a donut. Nobody else came in. Then I went to the nurses' station for our staff meeting. Everybody on our shift was there. I would guess that it ended about 7:15. Then I had to go back to my locker to get the protective clothing I wear because I'm caring for our messy patients. Do you know about that?"

"Yes, please go on."

"Miss Rice was just ahead of me and got her apron and gloves from her locker. I got into my protective wear and then sat on the bench in the hall for about ten minutes and read from a romance novel that I had in my locker before I started my rounds. I didn't see anybody, but just before I left, someone started to open the door from the ward but then changed their mind."

"Did you see who it was?"

"No, I was reading and didn't look up."

"What color is your bathing cap?"

"It's white."

"What about the other girls?"

"Helga has a blue cap, but I'm pretty sure that all the others that I've seen are white like mine."

"Okay, what happened then?"

"My first two patients were on the two corridors between the main entrance and the nurses' station. Are you familiar with the layout of the Violent Ward?"

"Yes."

"Okay. That took at least ten minutes. While I was attending to them, I saw Miss Rice, Helga, and Andy who were taking care of patients in that area, but I can't give you precise times."

"Was Helga wearing her bathing cap?"

"No. Since I handle all the messy patients now, she only uses it when she's showering patients."

"Helga said that she didn't see you. Are you sure that you saw her?"

"Yes. She's distinctive as a very tall blonde. She probably didn't see me because her back was to me as both of us were putting out bedpans."

"Okay, then what did you do."

"My next patient was in the little group of four rooms behind the nurses' station. Mrs. Greene was at the station. As I walked around it, Andy was going into the corridor where Nora was being kept. While I was there, I talked with Mrs. Strickland for a few minutes. When I left for my last patient who was on Nora's corridor, Miss Rice and Andy were a little ahead of me, and I saw them go into what must have been Nora's room."

"What do you mean by that phrase?"

"I was a little surprised to see them go in there because I thought it was empty. Mrs. Greene didn't say anything about Nora during our briefing, but I'd guess that she discussed her with Andy when she pulled him aside after the meeting."

"Now, let's talk about you a little. How long have you worked here?"

"A month and a half."

"Did you have experience working in a mental hospital?"

"No. After graduating from high school, I worked five years as a secretary in a doctor's office in Milwaukee. Then, this May the doctor's wife caught him fondling me in his surgery, so I was ruined there. My mother had gone to nursing school with Miss Mason, and they had kept in touch. Mom knew about the nurses' aide program here and thought that it would be a good chance for me to start over where nobody knew me. She contacted Miss Mason, and everything worked out."

"Why would a novice be put on the Violent Ward? Isn't it the most difficult assignment at the hospital?"

"Miss Mason told me that she was putting me there because there had been several sudden vacancies. She thought I could handle it because I had very good grades in high school and seemed mature in my telephone interview. Also, she said that, since I came from so far away, I couldn't be linked to the scandals in the ward."

"Well, you might look at it the other way. Since nobody here knows you, you might have some unsavory connections."

"If you have any doubts, here's a telephone number that I've written down where Mr. Williams can vouch for me."

"We'll check you out as soon as we can but thinking ahead to prepare this makes me think that you're not a naïve young lady. We need to keep you in custody until you're cleared. Do you understand?"

"Yes. I'm sure you'll get a quick answer."

"For your sake, I hope you're right. Laura, here's the telephone number. Please see if she checks out. Then call Bridget to escort her to the same cell that Helga's in. Tell her to escort Bertha up for questioning when she brings the shackles for Kathy."

Chapter 8 ~ Who's a Naughty Nurse?

There was little conversation until Bertha replaced Kathy in the hot seat.

"Hello, Mrs. Bartholomew. I hope seeing Miss Steele put in shackles didn't upset you. We have to keep her in temporary custody until we verify that she's who she says she is."

"No, sir. I certainly have a clean conscious."

"We need to figure out who was where on the Violent Ward before 7:45. Could you please tell us what you know?"

"I got to the ward about 6:40, bringing a big plate of donuts from the cafeteria with me. I went into the kitchen with my friend Sheila Mills, who's an attendant on the night shift, and got the coffee started. We chatted until about ten to seven. Sheila left to check in with her charge nurse at the end of their shift and I went back to my locker to get the rubber gloves that I use for handling bedpans when I wake my five patients. While I was opening my locker, Miss Rice walked by going into the ward. I then went to the nurses' station, but nobody was there except for Mrs. Greene who was just coming out of the administrative suite, so I went back to the kitchen for another mug of coffee. By the time that I brought the coffee back to the nurses' station, most of the people were there. The meeting started a couple of minutes later when Helga, Andy, and Robert came up.

"After the meeting, I took my mug back to the kitchen to refill it and then went to check my pigeonhole in the nurses' station. When I got there, I saw Miss Rice walking down the corridor that goes back from the left side of the station. She was wearing a rubber apron and gloves, which I thought was a little strange because we wouldn't start waking the patients for another ten-fifteen minutes and she usually wouldn't be in an apron. My pigeonhole was empty, so I went back to the kitchen for a donut. Helga was there as well. Then I started waking up my patients at 7:30. I started with the two who were in the corridor where Nora's cell was because everyone else starts elsewhere. I didn't see anyone when I was tending them. I then went to the rooms behind the nurses' station where I have one patient. Mrs. Greene was sitting at the nurses' station as

I went past. I tended to my patient there. By then I'm sure it was 7:45. As I was leaving her room, I saw Kathy Steele walking away from me."

"Thank you, Bertha. That's very helpful. Could you tell us where the corridor that you saw Miss Rice walking along goes?"

"Of course, sir. First, you come to the entry to a group of four patient rooms. Then there's the maximum-security area. After that, there's another corridor that goes off at a right angle to the left behind the day room and lounge, with the medicine cabinet and storerooms opening off it. Finally, the side exit to the ward is at the end of the hallway."

"Well, that's good. I've got one final question. Did you see Andy in the dining room?"

"Yes, sir. He was sitting on the far side of the room facing the other way when I went back to the kitchen and munching a donut. When I left to go on duty after chatting with Helga, he was gone."

After Bertha's departure was signaled by a door opening and closing, Detective Perkins told Laura to bring Michelle Rice up in shackles because she looked very suspicious. After she left, Detective Kempton expressed some optimism. "Well, Richard. Maybe, we're finally getting somewhere. The night crew didn't seem suspicious, but the information the day shift gave us was confusing and pointed in contradictory directions. Now, this last gal has got some serious explaining to do. The one we've arrested seems to be up to her ears in smuggling in the contraband, but it would have been too dangerous for her to try to sneak things in to Nora when she had no business being on the ward. Let's hope that we can go home with a clean conscience and another prisoner in tow, even if I'm a little disappointed that Helga's story was corroborated."

Detective Perkins laughed. "I hope you're right, Matt, but the more I hear, the less certain I am about what was going on down there this morning. Do you want to go looking for coffee?"

"No, that's okay. Let's hope we break this one quickly and can stop off at Bud's Bar while the girls haul her to jail."

They both laughed. There were several minutes of silence and then the door opened, and we heard what sounded like several sets of light footsteps come in before the door closed again. Detective Perkins sounded surprised. "Hello, ladies. It's always good to see you, but where is our suspect? Please, don't tell me she's been able to run away, too."

Officer Devlin answered quickly. "No, sir. Of course not. One of us has had her under direct observation since we got here. We need to confer for a few minutes about two things, so Susan is holding her out in the secretaries' office. They're getting quite an eyeful of that chained-up nurse. First, a messenger brought a letter for Laura from police headquarters. Do you want to open it?"

"No, Bridget. Since it's addressed to her, please give it to her. She can have the honor of opening it and telling us what's it about, unless it's confidential, of course."

"I don't have any secrets from you, Richard. I'm sure I'll be happy to read it to you, unless I'm being fired. Oh, it's signed by Chief Richardson. Let me read it.

"Dear Officer Sanders. Miss Katherine Steele is not, let me repeat not, a suspect in the case that you are investigating. In approximately an hour Mr. John Williams will call you at Elm Hill to verify Miss Steele's identity. Thus, she should be released immediately. Do not discuss this matter with anyone else except your investigative team, even members of the force.

"That's pretty clear. But why would we need a call from Mr. Williams when we've already got this?"

Detective Perkins laughed heartily. "What I really like about you, Laura, is that you can still be naïve after four years' of police work. Chief Richardson obviously doesn't want Miss Steele linked to him or the police. Elm Hill's eavesdropping operators can probably be trusted to satisfy any nasty snoop that we verified her identity through normal channels. Now, Bridget, what else do you have for us?"

"We searched the lockers, sir. We found Helga's blue cap in her locker and white caps in Bertha's, Kathy's, Michelle's, and Andy's. Surprisingly, Jane Greene had a yellow cap and swimsuit, although Michelle has never seen her use them in the three years that she has worked on the Violent Ward. I took the cap to Helga in her cell. She confirmed that it was hers by a small stain on it. As I was turning to leave, however, she asked to see the cap again and said that something was strange. She claimed that she always snapped her chin strap on and off on the left side. In contrast, the cap was unsnapped on the right."

"Did you check who has access to those lockers?"

"Yes, sir. According to the woman who's the acting charge nurse for the rest of the shift, the nurse manager and all the charge nurses have master keys, but so do a variety of hospital administrators as well, so it's going to be hard to narrow down who could have gotten a key."

"That's very good work, Bridget. Unfortunately, I think you're right about the practicality of tracing who has access to the lockers. When they planted drugs and pornography in June, they even got a key to Miss Mason's office."

"Thank you, sir. It's not often that a superior is complimentary to one of us. What should we do now?"

"You should get the prisoner, and Laura should go down to the nurse manager's office to wait for the call from Mr. Williams. Bridget, please stay for the interrogation."

Once Bridget had brought Miss Rice in, Detective Perkins sounded quite formal as he began to question her. "Miss Rice, you were taken into custody after several witnesses raised serious suspicions about you. If you can explain things to our satisfaction, you'll be released, but if you don't, you'll be arrested and transported to the Osloville Jail. You must tell us the exact truth and not try to hide anything. Think very carefully and don't try to lie. Do you understand?"

"Yes, sir. I really don't have anything to hide."

"It's very important that we establish who was doing what up to 7:45. Please describe what you did and who you saw after you got to the hospital."

"I got to the hospital about 6:45. As I was walking through the entry hall, I saw Bertha. When I got to the nurses' station, there was nobody there, but the door was open to the nurse manager's suite. I saw the back of Molly Wells in the doorway. She was talking to someone further inside. I'd guess that it was Mrs. Greene and that they were going through the shift changeover. Since nobody from our shift was around, I went to the lounge and read magazines until a couple of minutes before seven.

"During the meeting, I pulled a note out of my pigeonhole asking me to check our inventory of enema bags. We've had several new patients and are expecting a couple more admissions. In addition, maybe because the summer heat is causing tempers to fray, we're getting more temporary patients for a week or two. Our nurse manager is a firm believer in using enemas for constipation, so she well might have been worried that we might need five or six pretty quickly. I went to my locker to get a rubber apron and gloves because the bags are kept in a grubby back corner of our storeroom, and I like to keep my uniform looking fresh and professional. I then went back to the storeroom and checked the inventory. There were only two bags that were in the regular place. I took a few minutes to look around the storeroom, fruitlessly I might say, and then went to the nurses' station where I left a note for Mrs. Greene asking her to order a dozen more. I started to go back to the entry hall to put my apron in my locker but then decided that I might as well keep it on. Since Miss Weymouth's room is by the main entrance, I started my rounds by taking care of her. She's just starting two weeks in the Violent Ward, so she had lots of questions for me. By the time we had finished, Andy came to get me to search Nora and her cell. I'm sure one or two people were around when I put out Miss Weymouth's bedpan, but I didn't pay any attention to who they were."

"Did you open the door to the entry hall before you changed your mind?"

"Yes, sir."

"Okay, now we need to discuss some details. Did Mrs. Wells see you when you walked past her?"

"I doubt it. Her back was to me, and she seemed to be deep in conversation."

"Did you see anyone else from the night shift?"

"No, sir. Their lockers are by the side exit, and most of them were probably there by the time I got to the ward."

"So, there's nobody who can confirm that you went to the lounge?"

"No, there was nobody else around."

"Well, that's a problem for you, isn't it?"

"Why?"

"Instead of reading magazines, you could have just as easily have turned left and given Nora a threatening note."

"Is that why I'm in chains?"

"That's one reason. What about the note about the enema bags? What did you do with it?"

"I crumpled it up and threw it in the wastebasket by the nurses' station."

"Was the note from Mrs. Greene?"

"I think so. Let me think a moment. It was printed, so I'm not sure. The order could have come from Miss Rayburn to Mrs. Greene, and she could have just passed it on to me."

"Now, let's talk about your expedition in search of enema bags. Do you know what that nasty Nora did to Mrs. Greene?"

"No, sir."

"Instead of going to breakfast, she went to the nurses' station and asked Mrs. Greene for a sedative. When they went to the medicine cabinet to get a dose, she grabbed a scalpel that had been left there for her. Then she used it to subdue Mrs. Greene, steal her clothes, and leave her straitjacketed and gagged. By your own admission, you had plenty of opportunity to secret the scalpel since the big storeroom is right next to the pharmacy room. Now, do you have anything to add?"

"No, sir. I can't. I know it looks bad, but I did just what I said."

"Who on your shift has a key to the medicine room?"

"Just Mrs. Greene and myself, as well as Miss Rayburn. Only nurses can handle and dispense medicine."

"I'm sorry, Miss Rice, but the circumstantial evidence is quite strong. Therefore, I'm arresting you on suspicion of aiding and abetting the aggravated assault on Mrs. Greene. Bridget, you and Susan should transport her to headquarters. Get her booked. We'll resume questioning later today. Have Laura bring Helga back up here, but she doesn't need to keep her shackled."

Once the women had left, Detectives Perkins and Kempton exchanged jovial comments and congratulations over their arrest. Laura returned with Helga in just a couple of minutes, and Detective Perkins was quick to reassure her.

"Hello, Helga. I've got good news for you. We arrested Michelle Rice who has much more that she can't explain than you do. In addition, the way the woman in the blue cap drew attention to herself seemed a little contrived to me. We're releasing you."

"Oh, thank you sir. I'm so relieved. I'm sure my parents would have been heartbroken if I had been sent to jail. I really feel sorry for Miss Rice. She was nice to us for a 'black band.' Really, she seemed too nice to be wicked."

"What's a black band?"

"That's what we aides and the attendants call the nurses because of the black stripes on their caps showing that they're RN's."

"There's one more thing, Helga. I'm confining you to Elm Hill. There's still some suspicion about you, so I don't want you running away or getting in touch with criminals. If you're seen outside of the hospital grounds, you'll be arrested."

"I understand, sir. Really, after what you've just said, I'm afraid to go into town."

Once Helga left, Detective Perkins expressed satisfaction with the day's work.

"I really feel good about sending that second nurse to jail. I think that it's significant that she admitted to opening the door into the locker room."

This seemed to puzzle Detective Kempton. "Why? I don't see anything in it. She still was in her apron when we interviewed her."

"It's not the apron that's relevant. I was thinking that whoever opened the door just before 7:30 might have been on her way to put Helga's blue cap back in her locker. Michelle's certainly a good candidate, especially since she has a master key."

With their business concluded, Detective Perkins said that he'd treat the other two to beer and burgers at Bud's Bar. Laura tapped on Miss Mason's door a couple of minutes later.

"Come in. I see your lipstick is smudged. Have you been kissing your fiancé?"

The policewoman blushed. "Yes, ma'am. I think that we had a very successful afternoon, and I just wanted to celebrate. Richard asked me to tell you that we've arrested Michelle Rice on suspicion of helping Nora. I hope you agree. She seems by far the most likely one to have given the note and scalpel to her."

"I think that jail's the best place for her, just like Rachel Weiss. Let's hope that you can apprehend Nora as well and find out what's really going on. I think that what we heard was quite suggestive about who might be a naughty nurse, but let's hope that the police can tie up their investigation quickly."

"Richard will be pleased that you agree with him. Well, I've got to go. Andy, do you want to come with me? I got a message that Nell is arranging a search by the river. We can stop by Brackman's basement to get our hip boots and drive down to the park."

Chapter 9 ~ Confirmatory Evidence

When we reached the park, we found six women. I recognized Officers Devlin and Hastings. After we pulled on our boots and got out of the police cruiser, Laura introduced me to two blondes in chest waders who, like Officer Hastings, were from the swing shift that had been assigned to help Detective Perkins with the case. The older one, Evangeline Bartlett, was in charge of the operation as the senior policewoman on site. The other, Alice Prentice, was taller and tougher looking. In addition, there were two girls in their late teens, meter maids Jean and Becky who seemed quite excited about being included in real police work. Following the introductions, Officer Bartlett organized our search.

"Thanks so much for volunteering. Nell came to me with the idea of doing a more thorough search of where the fugitives went, and I've organized this. She suggested that we pair off, so that those of us, who like me, don't have much experience with waders can be helped by someone who does if they start stumbling. Bridget and I will be together, Alice will partner with Laura, Nell will take care of Andy, and Jean and Becky are both outdoorswomen. Nell has over-the-elbow rubber gloves for you. I'd suggest that you carry them until you need them."

We formed a line with four of us on each side of the tracks. I noticed that Officers Devlin and Prentice held their partners' arms, while Officer Hastings trusted me to walk without falling. Laura joked that this reminded her of trying to walk in heels.

After ten-minutes, we came to a spot where a small spring had created a muddy basin. Officer Hastings, who was walking nearest to the tracks, stopped at its edge. "Hey, I see something that I missed when I went on the other side. Let's hope it's their trash. Andy, would you please get it for us? Let me pull your gloves on for you. It's awkward when you do it yourself."

I came up next to her. Two sets of tracks went straight across the basin and passed a heavy-looking log that was on the other side of the from us. A piece of balled white paper was sticking out from under it. Officer Hastings held my arm as we stepped down into two inches of mud and then followed me effortlessly. Fortunately, the part of the log in the basin was from the top of the tree. Still, we couldn't roll it. In the end, I got down on hands and knees and poked my way through the branches to retrieve the paper. Officer Hastings pulled me back to my feet and once we were back on solid ground, she uncrumpled the paper, read it, and handed it up to Officer Bartlett.

"Well, girls and Andy, we haven't wasted our time. Here's a map and instructions of how to get from the nearby park to the door between the tunnels and the hospital. Then it ends with the same warning that Nora received: IF YOU SQUEAL, YOU'LL DROWN LIKE A RAT."

"Thanks for getting this. It must have been gross down in the mud. This really sounds like the Griggs gang. Do you think that the handwriting is the same as in Nora's note?"

"No, it's significantly neater."

Nothing further occurred until we reached the river. Officer Bartlett had us form a line going outward from the bank, and my partner took a firm grip on my arm. We waded very slowly down the Muskrat. Fortunately, the water was clear. There was a surprising amount of debris, and by the time that we had gone fifty yards everyone had donned gloves and picked up something. In all, we made three discoveries that might be relevant. First, Office Devlin found a discarded purse which held Mrs. Greene's driver's license. Second, Officer Prentice spotted a box by the mental grate going into the tunnels. It had evidently been left by the people who had been bringing contraband into the hospital, who presumably had left in a hurry when Nora screamed. The giggling women passed several magazines around, but Laura threatened to handcuff me if I tried to steal a peak. Finally, the sharp-eyed Officer Hastings found a women's watch with a broken wrist band.

Later, I agreed to have supper with Clem. When I got to the cafeteria, he waved me over to a table in a semi-deserted corner. He was sitting with a stocky Hispanic who seemed to be in his early 60s. I got my food and joined them.

"Hi, Andy. This is Frank Ramos, my friend of thirty or more years. Frank, this is Andy Russell from State U. who's working for Miss Mason."

We shook hands, and Clem continued.

"Frank, I'd sure you've heard about our adventure in the tunnels this morning. I thought maybe you could help us make sense of what we saw. For example, I guessed that they were built from the Brackman cellar down to the river early in Prohibition."

"I see you remember that I used to work in the old Rabbit Hole. You're right, as you usually are. The Brackman Department Store was big and profitable dating back to the turn of the century. Old man Brackman was rich and friends with the mayor when Prohibition hit here in 1920. This was a pretty religious community back then, so the bars were shut down. Mr. Brackman saw a great opportunity to make a mint as a bootlegger. He had the contacts in Canada and enough dough to buy the booze in large quantities and to make the necessary payoffs to his political friends. He brought the liquor up from the river to his house and sold it from there to the Griggs gang who ran the speakeasies. They probably would've liked to cut him out as a middle man, but he was too well connected. I had it on pretty good authority that they tried to lean on him in 1923 or 1924, but then the Police Chief himself made a personal visit to Chris Griggs and that ended that. You can't really hide speakeasies in a town this size, and the threat to have the cops come in and smash them up with axes was pretty intimidating, even to that vicious criminal."

"Did you hear that the old bootlegger tunnel was extended to the hospital, presumably when we were building it? Do you have any idea what happened?"

"Well, I was very glad to hear that I'm off the hook for letting Naughty Nora slip away. I can't help you about the new tunnel, however. We both worked on the hospital construction, but I didn't hear any gossip about tunnels or smugglers. Reynolds Construction certainly had some shady connections even back then, so they were probably behind it. I have no idea what it was done for, however. Do you have any idea what Nora was up to?"

"I wish I did. Andy caught her sneaking back in last night. What I can't figure out is why she just didn't say that she was making love to some not-too-desirable young man. She certainly was dressed for it from what I've heard about what was found in her bag. I'm sure Miss Mason would have had her scrubbing out toilets for a couple of weeks, but that's small potatoes compared to the trouble she's in now."

The two old friends traded several jocular stories and concluded that all was well with security at the front gate. As our conversation was winding down, a pretty woman attendant who looked as if she were just out of high school approached Clem.

"Mr. Jones, is it true that Nora was doing something wrong last night?"

"Well, we don't know what she was doing Tuesday night before Andy here caught her sneaking in, but she certainly was bad enough this morning to get sent to the Crawford State Prison for Women for several years if they catch her."

"I think I saw something suspicious yesterday. Both of us work the morning shift in Ward 2. At the end of the shift, I saw her coming out of the medicine cabinet just a couple of minutes before three. She was obviously leaving the ward because she had her purse, so she couldn't have been getting medication for anyone."

"Thanks so much for telling me about this, Maria. I'm glad you're keeping your eyes open. I don't see how she could be stealing from there, however. Do you? The inventories in the medicine cabinets have to be reconciled with what was given out to patients weekly. I think that some wards do it daily. My impression is that Mrs. Lawrence, your nurse manager, is very meticulous. I don't think that sneaky little nurse could draw the wool over her eyes. However, if you have suspicions or concerns in the future, please let me know right away. I'll pass this on to Miss Mason but not mention any names. Even if there's the faintest chance that somebody has figured out how to beat our drug control system, she should know."

Maria looked pleased to get praise from her supervisor. "Thank you, sir. I certainly will. I agree that it probably couldn't be done, but with everything they're saying about her, who knows what she was up to?"

After she left, I asked Mr. Jones what he thought. He seemed more serious than I had expected. "She's one of the good new attendants, a really sweet and responsible girl. I didn't want to get her wind up with so much gossip going around, but there's a chance that Nora might have been raiding the drug supply. Especially in Ward 2 where it's so hard to make many of the patients take their medications, you could squirrel away a significant amount without raising suspicion just by not forcing prescriptions down a few old ladies' throats. Also, she could've gotten placebo pills and substituted them for the real drugs in the medicine cabinet. I'm sure that Miss Mason and Mrs. Lawrence will check into things, but they need to do so very quietly."

After supper, I walked back to the dormitory and was surprised to see a police car pulled up next to the gate to the backyard of Brackman Hall. I had to use that gate to get into my basement room. Laura got out of the driver's side and took several steps towards me that seemed a little hesitant.

"Hi, Andy."

"Hi, Laura. I hope I'm not in trouble."

"No, of course not. I have to check Rachel's boot against the prints in the tunnel. I'd like you to come with me to see for yourself."

"Okay, although I'd certainly take your word for anything. I really would."

"Well, let's get going. Clem and Nell left all the protective wear that we used this morning in the cellar. Let me get Rachel's boots and a kit for making a plaster cast of the footprint from my trunk.

She checked me thoroughly as we donned our rubber wardrobes to make sure that I was completely covered, reminding me a little of Officer Hastings. As she snapped my rain helmet into place, she looked at me with a strange expression that was both tender and wary.

"Andy, do you hate me?"

"Why would I hate you? I thought we were friends."

"Well, I did arrest your girlfriend today. The way you were holding hands during her interrogation almost made me jealous. Are you really sure you're not angry with me about her?"

"Yes, I'm sure. Rachel even told me when you went out to Mrs. Holdstrom's office that you treated her professionally. It's very hard for me to believe that that sweet girl is mixed up with a criminal gang, but I can't fault your investigation."

"Furthermore, I noticed you reacted strangely when I handled you. What about Bridget Devlin and Nell Hastings? They had you in handcuffs and put you through a strip search. Or, are they okay because they're younger and cuter?"

I blushed and told her that she was just as pretty as they are.

"Thanks so much. However, being in custody makes many people unhappy with the police."

"I did feel humiliated, but I know that they had to do it. I certainly don't feel mad at you. You were just doing your duty. I must admit, however, that being in their custody brought home why I'm a little afraid of you. What did Officers Devlin and Hastings say about me?"

This made Laura giggle. "They said that you were a good boy and very cooperative, although Nell thinks that you don't respect our authority enough. They were surprised that you weren't wearing a girdle and nurse's stockings. It's a misery loves company thing because policewomen, but not men, are required to be tightly girdled. Don't think about asking Bridget out, however, at least until this case is closed. She's nice, but she plays it by the rules. I'm sure that in her view you're still a suspect. Also, perhaps I should warn you, she's quite a marksman, better than most of the male cops, which embarrasses them. As for Nell, she likes to dominant men. The male cops despise her. They claim that she handcuffs her boyfriends when they're making love, but that might just be malicious gossip. All I know is that she's twenty-three with no hint of wedding bells."

"Well, you make Officer Hastings seem a little scary, but I don't think that Officer Devlin and you are like that."

"Thank you, Andy. I feel relieved that we're still friends. Well, I've got two good pieces of news for you. First, we're going to be Black Angels again. Mrs. Holdstrom is going to have a dinner for us on Friday. Second, I haven't seen you for a while, so this is my first chance to tell you that your sister Jennifer is staying with me next week. Once my brothers moved out of our house, we've had plenty of room for guests. She's really enthusiastic about my police work and eager to meet my father who's a retired cop."

I hadn't heard anything about the possibility of this visit since early June, so I was a little surprised. Jennifer, an incoming freshman at State U., had been much more popular than I was in high school but had not exactly been a diligent student. I had assumed that she would follow the same course in college, but now I started to wonder what her fascination with the police set off by a chance meeting with Laura might portend.

Luckily, we had reached the room by the river with boot tracks in the muddy floor, so I could avoid a complicated conversation about my sister. Laura, for her part, took charge of our operation.

"Stand here, Andy, and shine both our flashlights where I'm pointing. See, this is Rachel's left boot. The gum is in the middle of the heel, just like the mark in the mud. Now, we just need to make a plaster cast and check whether the boot fits it. Look, it slips in perfectly.

"I'm sorry, Andy, but your girlfriend seems to be headed for Crawford State Prison. Richard thinks that she probably went out and met the smugglers in this room since she would have needed hip boots to go any further and was right behind Nora when you caught her. Then, when you dragged Nora up to see Miss Mason, she scuttled back to the hospital through the tunnels. When she came home at two, she probably put the boots in a bag to bring them into the dormitory. No wonder she didn't think to clean them off. We've posted notices in Brackman asking if anyone saw her then, but we haven't heard anything yet."

Chapter 10 ~ An Unruly Morning

The next morning, we all arrived at the Violent Ward at 6:45 because Mrs. Greene wanted to spend more time than usual discussing organizational matters. Despite Miss Rayburn's good intentions of trying to keep our scandal from the patients, the absence of the popular charge nurse from the 3-to-11 shift yesterday made that impossible. The patients had continued to be confined to their rooms. In the late afternoon, Miss Rayburn, accompanied by a brawny male attendant, went to tell each patient individually that Nora had assaulted Mrs. Greene and that Miss Weiss and Miss Rice were being held by the police on suspicion of helping her. As I had learned firsthand earlier in the summer, such a situation greatly raised tensions on the ward as frightened patients became hostile and aggressive.

Mrs. Greene said that she wanted to move the ward back toward normal functioning but with very strict safeguards. Since it was Thursday, the patients needed to be showered. However, for safety's sake, instead of being showered in groups, they were taken individually from their cells to the showers and then back again with two staff members accompanying them to prevent any opportunity for conflicts and fights. The patients would also be encouraged to take hydrotherapy by soaking in full tubs, which meant that we would have to have several shifts in the tubs during the morning. She also told us to spend extra time with our patients when we were getting them up if we thought that we could reassure and calm them down. If we did see a patient becoming too agitated or aggressive, however, we should tell her immediately so that she could have them "packed," that is, wrapped tightly in wet sheets. Finally, because the threat of patient rampages, Mrs. Greene ordered us to don full protective wear throughout our shift and emphasized the point by buckling on her own yellow bathing cap. She then concluded the meeting by introducing the nurse who was replacing Michelle Rice. "This is Mrs. Velma Walters who's coming to us from Ward 3."

"Hi, everybody. I worked here about eight years ago and then transferred out. A few of my old patients are still here. So, I'm at least a little familiar with what goes on, and having to get into protective wear doesn't intimidate me. Also, it sounds like I should be helpful today because I'm an old hand at packing."

I went to Jenny Sachs as soon as the staff briefing was finished. Even though it was about ten minutes before we would normally start waking patients up, I thought that she might be in need of attention. Jenny was our most notorious patient who had been committed to Elm Hill after stabbing her husband, the current Secretary of State who was running for governor next year, in a fit of rage brought on by his brutish treatment of her. As a result, she was heavily restrained and feared by many of the patients and the staff, albeit with very little reason as far as I could tell. When I reached her room, I saw that, as I had suspected, she had spent the night in six-point bed restraints, wrist and ankle cuffs and straps across her tummy and thighs, which, in turn, necessitated heavy cloth diapers with locking rubber pants over them. She was almost cheerful, however, as I got her out of all of that.

"Hello, Mr. Russell. I see that they have you back in your cap, mask, and apron again. That's probably a good idea given how upset people are. I appreciate how considerate you are of me. It's good to have those wet diapers off. I guess one advantage of them, however, is that I don't have a messy bedpan this morning.

"Is it true what they said about Miss Weiss? I can't believe it. She's so nice."

"The police found some incriminating evidence linking her to Nora, but she says she's innocent. I really hope that she is."

I then told her about the changed arrangements for showering and recommended that she take hydrotherapy.

"That's a good idea. I do find that hydrotherapy is calming. It looks like I'll be in my rubber harness most of the morning. Have you ever seen it?"

"No, I don't go in the showers and don't remember seeing you in hydrotherapy. I guess it makes sense that you can't wear your regular restraining belt in the showers or the tubs."

"Will I have to be strait-jacketed when you exercise me?"

"Given the heightened security, I think I'd better do it. Jenny, do you feel upset?"

"I'm sad for Miss Weiss, but I'm certainly not going to attack anyone. You know I stabbed Rodney in a fit of rage, but I'm not angry at anyone here after the sadistic Amy and Thomas left. Don't worry. You won't have any trouble with me."

I decided to go to Valerie Waller next. She had come to the Violent Ward on the previous Thursday for a two-week temporary confinement because she had become too out-of-control on Ward 3. On Friday when I first took care of her, she had seemed quite subdued. When I came back on duty this Monday, however, she was in bed restraints, as she was on Tuesday and Wednesday. Indeed, she stayed in her room except for daily hydrotherapy. Consequently, I thought that yesterday's uproar might have affected her more than some of our patients, and this turned out to be the case.

Miss Waller was a high school junior. She was quick to note my extra protective clothing and asked if I had been told that she was a problem. As I was removing her restraints and diapers, I reassured her that we were just preparing for possible disturbances and asked her if she'd like to talk. This made her smile and nod eagerly.

I asked her to tell me about herself. Unlike most of the patients on the Violent Ward, she was able to describe herself and her situation quite coherently. She had been committed to the hospital in early May by her father, a well-respected physician in Springfield. Her parents claimed that she had started using drugs and was out of control. She claimed that she had gone to a few wild parties but that she had never used drugs and was maintaining good grades in school. The real reason for her committal, instead, was that she had started dating and having sex with a high school dropout who was from the wrong side of the tracks. One day when she returned home from school, she walked into the living room to find her mother close to tears and a uniformed policewoman. The policewoman quickly handcuffed her, told her that she had been committed to Elm Hill by her father, and took her to the toilet before the three-hour drive to Osloville.

Her first six weeks in Ward 3 were confusing and frightening, but she didn't have any major problems. There were two other girls on her ward who had also been sent there for being *wild*. One was a drug addict who seemed to be responding to treatment, while the other was waiting to be released at the end of the summer when she'd be sent to an out-of-state boarding school. Having concluded that she didn't want to continue her rebellious outburst, Valerie thought about writing to her parents to suggest a similar solution. However, before she could do anything, twin disasters struck. First, her psychiatrist, Dr. Sessions, informed her that her father was going to participate in her treatment and that he was scheduling her for a series of electro-shocks. Other patients told her that, while electro-shock helped many patients with conditions like depression and schizophrenia, none of the girls like her had been subjected to it for the last several years. They speculated that her father was trying to disrupt her short-term memory of her boyfriend. Second, she got into a tiff with Mrs. Rogers, the leader of a patient clique on the ward.

As a result, the Rogers' coterie began mocking and provoking Valerie just as she was being tormented by fears of electro-shock and of betrayal by her family. She then lost it after a well-aimed taunt by Mrs. Rogers about what her physician father was planning to do to her. Her uncontrolled screaming and pounding of Mrs. Rogers over the head with a couch cushion earned her a trip to seclusion. Being buckled into restraints for the first time by the nurse and female attendant who escorted her to the seclusion room then drove the poor girl over the edge. She recommended screaming and, even after being restrained on her belly, became, to quote the exasperated nurse, a "bucking bronco," which soon led to an injection of a strong sedative and a transfer her to the Violent Ward for two weeks. Luckily for Valerie, the charge nurse on duty in the Violent Ward when she woke up was Rachel Weiss, who had the patience to come to the seclusion room and calm her down before strait-jacketing her and wheelchairing her down to the basement where she was immediately packed.

Unfortunately, Mrs. Greene's premonition about chaos on the ward was soon fulfilled. After I took Jenny's breakfast to her in her room, I went to eat with my other patients. I had barely sat down when several women started screaming at one another, and soon a full food fight erupted. Luckily for us, it was dishes of food rather than full bedpans that were being tossed, but the result was a huge mess. My apron and cap got covered with scrambled eggs and breakfast potatoes. I was luckier than Kathy and Mrs. Walters, however, whose uniforms ended up soaked with coffee as well as food. In the aftermath, Mrs. Greene ordered that five of the most out-of-control women be packed and that all of our other sixteen patients be given hydrotherapy. In addition, she told me to use restraints on Valerie whenever she was out of her room, even though I was sure that Valerie had cowered in the corner during the uproar.

Chapter 11 ~ Return of the Black Angles

The next day the ward was tense, but there really weren't any violent outbursts. About half the patients received hydrotherapy, and two schizophrenics became so agitated that they were straitjacketed and taken to their rooms. Even with this improvement, I felt relieved and happy to finish my duties and look forward to dinner at the Holdstroms that night with a relaxing weekend to follow.

Miss Mason picked me up in front of Brackman at 6:45. We had a pleasant drive to the Holdstroms' home, chatting about inconsequential things. The two detectives, Laura, and Clem had also been invited. Mrs. Holdstrom's husband Peter and their two high-school aged children, Peter Jr. and Helen, were also there. As usual, their housekeeper Debbie made a sumptuous dinner, baked chicken, macaroni and cheese, green beans, rye bread, and blueberry pie. I sat next to Peter Jr., who was going to State U. as a freshman in the fall. We talked about university life, and I got a strong impression that he was far more studiously inclined than my sister Jennifer. When dinner was finished, Mrs. Holdstrom led us back to the library where a coffee service had been laid out.

Miss Mason greeted us more cheerily than she probably felt given the situation at Elm Hill. "Thank you so much for coming, although Debbie's cooking is certainly a reward in itself. Unfortunately, it's time to resurrect the Black Angels. Luckily, we don't have to wear our rainwear since there's hardly a cloud in the sky this evening. This time of a year a slicker might keep the outside of your clothes dry, but it would get the insides soaked quickly. Anyway, Richard, you asked to get us together, so, hopefully, that means that you've made some progress in your investigation."

"Well, I'm not sure about progress, but we've averted at least one disaster. I've brought tapes of the interviews that we had Wednesday evening with Mrs. Greene, the two nurses whom we arrested, and Rachel Weiss's roommate. None of them provide much new information, but they are consistent with the interviews that we did at the hospital, with which I'm sure at least Miss Mason is quite familiar. Let's start with Mrs.

Greene since we did her first." He turned on the tape recorder, and his voice started the interrogation.

"Are you feeling better, ma'am? I'm Detective Perkins. This is Officer Sanders who's with me. I know you've had a terrible experience."

"Thank you, Detective. I think that I'm okay now. I really wasn't that scared at the time, but now I'm a little humiliated that I let that girl get away."

"Don't feel bad about that, ma'am. If you hadn't cooperated, she might have hurt or even killed you. Your safety is what's most important. Now, could you please read what Miss Mason remembered of your description of the incident? If you think that it's complete and accurate, we won't need to probe about those horrible events."

After a brief pause, Mrs. Greene responded, "I can't think of anything else."

"Well, if something comes to mind later when you've had time to relax, just give me a call. Now, would you mind signing at the bottom to make it official? Here, let me give you a pen. What can you tell me about Nora?"

"I know that she's a nurse on Ward 2. I really have hardly anything to do with her. She's one of our younger and wilder ones, but I really didn't think that she could be so wicked."

"This may sound strange, but a question has come up about the rubber caps that everybody on your shift wears. Have you ever seen a blue one besides the one that Helga wears?"

"That's easy. The only other one that's colored is my yellow one."

"What about the other shifts?"

"I doubt that anyone on the night shift would need a cap. The evening shift would have to have somebody handle messy patients, and some of the staff might keep protective wear for when things get really wild on the ward. I'd guess that most or all of the women on the two swing shifts that work part-time on the Violent Ward would have caps because they have to sub for the daytime and evening shifts on a regular basis."

"Do you know what color the caps are?"

"No. Wait a minute. Rachel Weiss, the charge nurse on the evening shift, wore a red cap and suit when she showered patients on our shift before her promotion.

"Finally, we're trying to see who could have given the note to Nora and planted the scalpel in the medicine room. Thus, could you please go over whom you saw from the time you got to the ward until about 7:45?"

"Certainly, although I don't think that I saw anything suspicious. I got to the hospital at about 6:30 and went directly to the nurses' station to confer with Molly Wells, the charge nurse for the night shift. We went into the administrative suit for privacy, which we do about half the time, because she had to brief me about Nora's being locked up. I must admit that we did gossip a bit about what the stupid little twit had gotten herself into this time. Molly left just before seven. I relaxed for a few minutes and then went out for the morning meeting with the staff on our shift which lasted from a few minutes after seven until about 7:15. After the general briefing, I talked with Andy for a few minutes about Nora since he'd be the one caring for her. After he left, I stayed at the nurses' station. I saw just about everybody, but I really wasn't paying attention to who was doing what. Finally, Miss Rice reported that Andy had found a note that a staff member must have given to Nora, but that a search of the cell and full strip search of the patient hadn't turn up anything else."

"Did she tell you what the note said?"

"No. I just assumed that it was something silly or, given her reputation, that one of the night-shift attendants had propositioned her."

"Thanks so much. I've just got three short questions about details. First, did Mrs. Wells stand in the open door of the administrative suite and talk to you as she was leaving?

"Now that you mention it, she did. By then we were talking about much less sensitive matters than Nora."

"Second, did you leave a note in Miss Rice's pigeonhole, asking her to check the supply of enema bags this morning?"

"No, I didn't, but Miss Rayburn could have. She's a firm believer in proactive enemas."

"Finally, did you see anyone going toward the corridor to Nora's room before the staff started their rounds?"

"No. First, I was talking to Andy, and then I was behind the counter, so my vision was blocked in that direction."

Here, Detective Perkins stopped and removed the tape, said that he was moving on to the two prisoners, and slotted a new tape into the player.

"Hello, Michelle. Do you remember who we are? I'm Detective Perkins, and these are Detective Kempton and Officer Sanders. Laura, would you please sit by her? Since she's shackled, she'll need help if she wants a tissue or drink of water."

"I remember you, sir. Thank you for being so considerate."

"Have you thought about what you told us at the hospital? Is there anything that you'd like to add or change?"

"No, sir. I told you all I know."

"Have you talked to anyone about the case since your arrest?"

"The matron let me call my parents. My dad cried, and my mom said that she'd always told me I get in trouble if I went off with the lunatics. Both said that I should cooperate with you. When she was bringing me here, Matron Jenkins said that you were a good cop who usually got at the truth."

"Well, you should take their advice. Now, we have a few questions for you. You said that you were in the lounge for ten-to-fifteen minutes before the staff briefing. Is that correct?"

"Yes, sir."

"Do you remember whether the door to the lounge was open or closed?"

"It's always open."

"Could you see or hear whether anybody went into the corridor where Nora's cell was?"

"I certainly couldn't see from inside the lounge. I'm not sure about hearing. I was reading *Look* and not really on alert because all the patients were still locked in their rooms. I'm sorry, but I just don't know."

"We have one problem with what you told us earlier. Do you know what it is?"

"No, sir. Everything I told you was true."

"We looked in the trash at the nurses' station. There wasn't any note from Mrs. Greene or Miss Rayburn to you. Mr. Martindale said that the wastebasket hadn't been emptied after the morning briefing. So, we're wondering where it went."

"I don't know, sir. I definitely remember putting it in. Did you find my note to Mrs. Greene?"

"Yes, we did.

"Now, Michelle. We have to ask you some intimate questions, so we'll leave you with Officer Sanders to minimize the humiliation. I'm sorry but this is vital information to our investigation."

After the door open and closed, Laura started the questioning almost apologetically.

"Michelle, we just can't figure out why you would do such a horrible thing. One idea that the detectives had was that you might be having an affair with a doctor who got you involved in this criminal scheme. As you know, we arrested several girls from the Violent Ward in June for just that reason. I have to ask you about your sex life."

"Yes. ma'am."

"Are you having an affair with a doctor? Is that the reason that you're in trouble now?"

"No, ma'am. Look at me. I'm plain and 34. What doctor would want me? They don't even pat my bottom. I've had some discrete affairs with attendants, but that's all."

"Were you one of Thomas's girls? Is that how you got involved with this?"

"No, ma'am. He's a sadistic creep. I'd never get involved with him. Anyway, he liked them pretty, but also young and stupid. I know you don't believe me, ma'am, but really I'm innocent."

Detective Perkins stopped the tape and replaced it with another. It opened with Laura speaking.

"Hello, Rachel. Unfortunately, we must ask you some very intimate questions, so the detectives asked me to conduct this interview. Matron Jenkins is here as a witness.

"Let's start with a question that isn't sensitive. Have you talked with anyone since your arrest?"

"Yes, ma'am. I was allowed to call my parents."

"What did they say?"

"They were shocked. I think that they believed me when I said I was innocent, but I know they feel totally humiliated."

"Please listen, Rachel. You're not in anywhere as much trouble as Michelle. She's an accomplice to an aggravated assault and probably several other serious charges. All you've done is help bring some contraband into Elm Hill. If you plead guilty and tell us what was going on before we catch Nora, you'll just get a sentence in the jail here, like Carly. How can you expect us to believe that you'd be in the medical library until two in the morning? Are you afraid that the Griggs gang will kill you? I don't blame you if you're frightened."

"Please, ma'am. I know you don't believe me, but I really was in the library."

"Well, now we come to the embarrassing part. I believe Miss Mason when she says that there's no evidence that you're sexually active now, but we why would a clean-cut girl like you get involved in smuggling. We do know that several nasty doctors seduced nurses, aides, and female attendants over the last year and then got them involved in criminal activities. Did something like that happen to you Rachel? Do you have a crush on a doctor? Are you trying to impress him?"

"Oh, no ma'am. How could you think I'm so wicked?"

"So, you don't have any boyfriend?"

"No, ma'am."

"Then why wouldn't you go out with Andy? He seems nice enough. Really, I couldn't believe how supportive he was of you doing your interrogation. Do you want to be an old maid?"

"I'd love to get married, but Andy's going back to College City in a month. I don't want to have just an affair.

"Well, what would you do if you're sent to Crawford State Prison?"

"I know no decent man would want me after that. I'll go into a convent and hope they send me to nurse in a Catholic hospital."

Detective Perkins stopped the tape, ejected it, put in another, but gave us a brief explanation before starting it. "This is a brief interview that Laura had with Rachel's roommate, Shelley Newton, a nurse who works the day shift on Ward 5." He then pressed the start button.

"Hello, Miss Newton, I'm Officer Laura Sanders. Are you free for a few minutes? I need to ask you a few questions about your roommate."

"That shouldn't be a problem. The patients have just gone to their rooms after lunch for their naps. But what have you done with Rachel?"

"What do you know about her?"

"You went to her room, put her in chains, interrogated her in the administrative suite, and took her away."

"How would you know that? Weren't you here all morning?"

"How many people do you think saw you? They certainly didn't keep quiet about it."

"Okay, we need to know about what Rachel did last night."

"I'm sorry, but I don't think I can help you. I went to bed a little after ten. I woke for a moment when Rachel came in, but I have no idea what time it was. When I got up at six, she was gently snoring."

"Do you know what she did when she came in?"

"No, I just heard the door open and close and then rolled over and went back to sleep. She's quiet and very considerate.

"Is she a messy roommate?"

"Oh, no. She's very neat and tidy."

"What about her boots? Does she keep them nice and clean?"

"I'm pretty sure that she does, but I don't pay much attention to rainwear except when I need to use my own."

"Could you or Rachel confuse each other's boots?"

"No, ma'am. My feet are much bigger than hers. I'm sure that I couldn't get my feet into her boots."

By common consent we took a break when this last tape finished. We refilled our coffee cups as Mrs. Holdstrom went out to the kitchen and returned with a plate of chocolate-chip cookies. Detective Perkins then continued with a growing smile on his face.

"We had our fingerprint examiner, Phil Dutton, go over the crates that were found by the entrance from the tunnels into the hospital. Luckily for us, the smugglers and crooks in general don't lead the league in the brains department. He found fingerprints from Victor Buchanan, who runs the Griggs gang's drug operations, and another punk named Robertson. Based on that, I contacted my friend Ed Simms, the Lieutenant on the Vice Squad, who then flashed a picture of Nora around his contacts. Several of them said that for the last few months a woman who looks like Nora has been seen with Buchanan.

"We also followed up on Andy's suggestion that someone could have gotten out of the hospital grounds unseen early Wednesday morning by going through one of the side gates. There's a phone booth right across the street from one of them. We also checked the two cab companies. One of them got a call to pick up a fare at that booth at 12:49. The passenger, who had a laundry bag with her, wanted to go to the Robbers' Roost, one of Victor's prime hangouts. The woman was wearing dark clothing and a scarf and got into and out of the taxi in dark places, so the driver can't make any identification beyond saying that she was tall and looked big-boned. Unfortunately, we didn't have any informants there, and going down to ask questions would be a total waste of time and only tip Buchanan off that we know more about his business than he would want us to.

"Officer Bartlett had a good idea that might be relevant here as well. She and Andy found a note to Nora's accomplice that contained the same threat that Nora received earlier. Andy thought that the handwriting was much neater in this one. Evangeline suggested that it might have come from one of the gun molls at the Robbers Roost, which would be consistent with what we found out about the taxi.

"Our big news, however, is what I mentioned earlier, a potential disaster that didn't happen. After a Vice detective was caught in the fiasco of trying to plant contraband in Elm Hill in June, Ed Simms has had his two secretaries keep their eyes on several of that guy's buddies. The girls were quite enthusiastic about trying to get them in trouble because the creeps like to harass and humiliate women. Wednesday morning, Detective Dawson sent Barbara Knight to Judge Craven to get a search warrant as soon as he got to the office. Since Craven is pro-police and will sign anything, he hardly gave it a glance and sent her back to Vice where she found Dawson and two of his cronies ready to execute it. She had read it and was horrified to see that it was for Miss Mason's office, the office of Dr. Rydberg's two secretaries, and Andy's and Emma's lockers where, according to a highly credible informant, drugs and lesbian pornography had been hidden."

Here, there truly was a collective gasp, which made Detective Perkins smile. "Well, none of the targets have been arrested, so there's obviously nothing to worry about.

"Dawson shoved the warrant in Barbara's face and gloated, 'I'm sure you read this, you sneaky bitch. If you try to interfere, I'll arrest you, too. This is my ticket to taking over Vice. We'll make a big bust. In less than an hour we'll have them all in handcuffs. Once we make the arrests, the Chief, the State's Attorney, and the Mayor will have to back us and prosecute them to the hilt. Or, we'll bring them down for undermining the police. This is a conservative town, so the people won't stand for it.' Just then the telephone rang. Barbara picked it up. A hysterical woman demanded to talk to Dawson, and as Barbara held out the phone to him, they all could hear her scream, 'Abort. Abort.' Before you get worried about a dramatic coincidence, nothing would have happened even without the call. Barbara had alerted the Chief's office on her way back from city hall, and his top assistant waltzed in to read Dawson the riot act before Barbara could hang up the phone. What this really proves is that Victor and his cop cronies are pretty darn stupid, which I hope you find to be at least a little comforting."

Detective Perkins' bombshell certainly set off a good deal of chatter as people, depending upon their personality, expressed either outrage or relief. It also stimulated the warming up of coffee cups and nibbling of cookies. Finally, Miss Mason moved our meeting to the final stage.

"It's certainly been a wild day. From the Elm Hill end, we haven't found very much. An attendant on Ward 2 reported to Clem that Nora was acting suspiciously in the medicine closet as she was going off duty on the afternoon before she went cavorting through the tunnels. Given her later guilty actions, it worried Rebecca Lawrence, her nurse manager, and me quite a bit. She had gone over the medications room thoroughly last Thursday, and everything was balanced down to the last pill. Mrs. Lawrence is very responsible and precise, so she still wasn't satisfied. This morning she searched the medicine cabinet thoroughly. Each shelf is locked. They can only be opened individually. In Ward 2, there are several shelves at the bottom of the cabinet that haven't been used for years, if ever. Rebecca went through them and found four bottles of white pills, three of them full and one-half empty, suggesting that Nora may have been administering placebos and stealing our medications for her evil boyfriend. Here, I've got the bottles for you in this plastic bag, so you can search for fingerprints and test to see what's really in them.

Incidentally, I had Mrs. Lawrence wear gloves, so there's no need to fingerprint her. Unfortunately, we're getting far more experience with criminal investigations than we'd like.

"Other than that, I don't think that we turned up anything worthwhile. The half-brained plot to plant incriminating materials in Elm Hill, however, shows that there's still a plan afoot to take over the hospital. From what Richard says, this was a Keystone Cops fiasco initiated by a low-level gangster, but there must be some more powerful and dangerous people out there who still have some scheme going. I've got a meeting scheduled for us with Dr. Rydberg next Monday at three about what's going on at the hospital.

"Finally, the tunnels have been secured. Dr. Rydberg had the entrance from the river bricked up and new locks installed on the entrances from the hospital basement and Brackman Hall.

Chapter 12 ~ Captured

On Saturday evening, I went to a semi-pro baseball game with Clem. We had a good time, especially since Osloville won 5-2. Clem introduced me to several of the players before the game, so I had people to root for as individuals. After the game, we went to his house for dinner. I was looking forward to spending some time with his wife Ella because she was so personable, although his son and daughter were out on dates. When we got to his house, a woman called from the back,

"Clem, dear, is that you?"

"Who else would be walking in without ringing the doorbell? Andy's here with me."

"Thank heaven. Come back to our bedroom and lock the door behind you."

Clem locked and bolted the door and whispered to me, "Something's really wrong. Ella's not melodramatic. Stay out here. If I don't call you, Andy, go out the door and run to that blue house on the other side of the road. There are friends there."

He turned down the hallway leading to the back of the house from the living room and quickly called, "Come on back, Andy."

With at least a little trepidation, I went to the hall and saw him standing in a doorway at the far end. I followed him into a bedroom and got what was close to the shock of my life. His wife, tall, attractive, and a few years younger than he was, was sitting on a chair with a shotgun across her lap. A young woman in a dirty and torn brown dress was draped across the bed with her hands and feet tied together with a clothesline. It was Nora.

"Oh, Clem, when I got back from work a little before 6:00, I heard a noise in the basement. I don't think we have much worth stealing, but I took our shotgun down in case there was somebody there. She heard me coming down the stairs. When she saw who I was she put her hands in the air and started to cry. There're some terrible people who want to do her harm. That's why I'm sitting here with a gun to see if she was followed. I'll let her tell you her story herself."

"Please, ma'am. Before I start, may I use the toilet?"

Clem untied her ankles, and Ella took her to the bathroom. When she returned, Nora looked so frightened and exhausted that it was almost impossible to imagine her holding a scalpel to Mrs. Greene's throat. Clem then asked the obvious question.

"Whatever did you come here for, Nora? We're certainly not going to hide you from the police after what you did at Elm Hill."

"I don't have any place to go. The Griggs gang will kill me if they catch me because I know too much. If I'm put in jail, some crooked cops would probably do the same. I snuck into your basement last night through the coal chute, but then got afraid to give myself up to you in the morning. Now, all I know is that I can't go on."

"Tell us your problems, Nora, but I can't promise to do anything for you."

"About six months ago I met Victor Buchanan at a bar. He was really sexy, and I ignored a woman who told me to stay away from him because he was connected to some really questionable stuff. We had steamy sex which made me pretty happy. I'm ashamed to admit now. Then in mid-April, he told me that some of his friends wanted me to help them. If things worked out, I could make several thousand dollars for doing hardly anything. A week or so after the Adams murder, he had me come by his apartment and gave me a bottle full of white pills. He said that they were sugar pills and told me to give them to my patients instead of their medicine, which I was to steal and bring back to him. It didn't seem difficult since nobody inspects us when we go into or out of the hospital or the ward. In addition, most patients don't pay much attention to their medications. It was very easy."

"What happened then?"

"I went on stealing drugs for him for about four months. Then he got me involved in a new scheme. He was going to smuggle drugs and pornography into Elm Hill and have a few confederates like me plant them in sensitive places to get Dr. Rydberg, Miss Mason, and some of their staff arrested. Then some people working with the Griggs gang could take over the hospital and milk it for lots of money. He promised that I'd be promoted to a senior charge nurse."

"Do you know any of the other people involved in this scheme?"

"No, he said it was too dangerous for me to know any names."

"Was the night Andy caught you the first time you saw any smuggling?"

"Yes. That night, I met Victor at our usual bar, the Robbers' Roost. Then when we left the bar, he asked me whether I wanted to go on an adventure. Really, I wanted to go to his apartment, but clearly he had something else in mind. We drove to the park that's a little above Elm Hill and down to the cove. There was another car there. When we walked over to the other car, two burly guys got out, gave us slickers and boots, and quickly carried some boxes to a boat at the dock there. The boat had an outboard motor, but they used oars to push out into the current and row down to where the metal grate separates the river from the sewerage basin. Victor knew how to unlock and pull the screen back. We didn't talk or use our flashlights until we got into the little room beyond the basin. While his men were working with the boxes, he took me through the tunnels, first to the hospital and then a little further up the tunnel toward Elm Hill. He told me that the main tunnel was used by old man Brackman for smuggling during Prohibition and that the Griggs gang had built the side tunnel to the hospital when Elm Hill was constructed. Finally, he laughed, they were getting a chance to use it. When his men called to him, he went back and gave me two keys, one that was supposed to fit all the locks in the tunnel and one for the basement door in Brackman. Clem, did you explore the tunnel?"

"Yes, it goes from Brackman to the Muskrat River with a side passage to the basement of Elm Hill. Is that all of it?"

"That's all I saw, but there could be more."

"Did you see Rachel Weiss in the tunnels? Is she another one of Victor's girlfriends?"

"Don't be ridiculous. She'd be afraid of a real man like him. I certainly didn't see her. Why are you asking?"

The police found a footprint that they thought she'd made. They've arrested her."

"She's so 'goody-goody' that I've always despised her, but now I feel sorry for her. It's lucky Victor didn't catch her wandering around down there. I'm sure he would've killed her, wrapped her body in chains, and dropped it in the middle of the Muskrat."

"Well, Nora. You have a really sweat boyfriend.

"What happened the next morning? That's why you're really in trouble. I don't think that the police would have cared too much about a sightseer riding along with her boyfriend. Somebody must have helped you. Who was it? Aren't you ashamed of what you did to Mrs. Greene?"

Nora began to sob. "I know I was wicked. I know my life is ruined. But I was scared for my life! I know you probably won't believe me, but I never saw who came for me in the morning. The door to my cell opened slightly, and a gruff voice spoke through the crack demanding that I take off my gown and wrap it around my head. I was scared, but I did what I was told. I knew it couldn't be a regular hospital procedure, even in the Violent Ward. She came in and sat down next to me. Then she secured my hands behind my back with the padded handcuffs that we use. She told me that I had seen what I wasn't supposed to and that I had to disappear if I didn't want to be killed. Then she told me how to escape. After that she shoved the note into my hand, undid the handcuffs, and threatened to cut my throat if I took the gown off my head before she left."

"Are you sure it was a woman?"

"Actually, it sounded like a man, but I thought that it was a woman disguising her voice."

"How long was it after that when Andy came in?"

"I'm not sure. It seemed like a long time, but I was so frightened that I lost all track of time. It must have been at least half an hour and probably longer."

"We know you got down to the river through the tunnels. What happened then?"

"I was met by a woman with a light brown ponytail when I went into the tunnels from the hospital basement. She had these clothes for me, plus hip boots, and a slicker and rubber helmet to wear. She hustled me along to a car in the parking area at the end of the path and hid me in the trunk as she drove me to an abandoned farm house just south of town. she told me the Griggs gang had bought the place. She said that there was a little food there and that I shouldn't ever go outside or turn the lights on. I stayed in the basement where there was a small cot most of the time and only went upstairs to use the kitchen and bathroom. The next morning, which would have been Thursday, she came back to bring some more food and check that I was all right. She seemed a little tense in dealing with me and that made me scared. I was starting to realize that I didn't seem to have much future at the farm and that the Griggs gang is brutal. Then Friday evening well after dark, I was upstairs sitting on a couch in the living room and wondering what was to become of me, when I saw two cars turn into the long driveway and shut off their lights. I was scared, ran out the back of the house, and got away through the fields toward the river."

"Do you have any idea who was in the cars? Was it Victor and his gang members? What about the woman who rescued you?"

"I didn't wait to find out who was coming, and I'd never seen the woman before. I got the feeling that she might have felt sorry for me but couldn't afford to show any sympathy. Andy, do you remember that the note threatened to 'drown me like a rat?' When we came up from the river, Victor had pointed out the sewerage basin and said that the gang used it for their most gruesome executions. The victims would be gagged and chained to the bottom of the basin during the night when the pipes cleared out. Then they'd drown in the morning when the surge of sewerage from the hospital filled the basin. I was afraid that that was what they wanted to do to me."

"How did you get here? Why did you come?"

"I'm sorry if I put you in danger. I know I have to go to jail, but Victor had told me that some policemen work with the Griggs gang. I was afraid that I might be murdered if I got arrested in Osloville. I really didn't know what I could do when I was at the farm. I had overheard you once talking to my nurse manager, Mrs. Lawrence. I got the impression that you two were a lot friendlier than you let on in public. I thought that maybe you could put in a good word for me. Anyway, I really didn't have any place else to go, so I came here staying off the roads as much as I could after I got your address from a phone book in a telephone booth. I got here about four this morning. I was going to give myself up when you woke up, but then I got frightened."

"Are you hungry, Nora? It sounds like you've haven't eaten for the last day or so."

"Yes, Mr. Jones. I'm very hungry."

"Ella, why don't you start supper? Andy, stay in here with her and make sure she doesn't get up to any more tricks."

Nora, even with her hands bound tightly behind her back, fell back on the bed and dropped off to sleep almost immediately. In less than ten minutes, Clem opened the door and beckoned me with his hand. We than walked out to the living room where he told me he was going to Elm Hill to meet Miss Mason. When I asked what she thought, he said that he hadn't said anything because he was afraid the switchboard operator might be listening in, so he asked if he could meet her because several attendants wanted to change their schedule next week. This was a ready ruse they could always use because somebody usually had something come up. A little later, Mrs. Jones brought in a hamburger, baked beans, and a salad for Nora and had to feed her since Clem had left strict instructions to keep her restrained.

Clem returned in about an hour. When he came into the bedroom, Nora gazed up at him with frightened eyes. He tried to smile reassuringly.

"You've got a very long ride tonight and tomorrow, Nora. You're going to be taken to a psychiatric hospital out of state and confined in an agitated ward under another name. You'll have to stay there for several years. Then you can start a new life."

"Will I be able to contact my family to let them know that I'm safe? I know that I've disgraced them, but I don't want them to think that I'm dead."

"I'm sorry, but that's not a good idea. If anyone's looking for you, we don't want even the barest hint that you might have found some sanctuary. Unless the Griggs gang and the crooked cops in Osloville are put away, we can't risk having any links to you that they might follow. For example, I don't have any idea where you're going to be taken."

When I got back to my room that night, I found a note under my door asking me to meet Miss Mason at the front porch of Brackman at 9:30 the next morning. She suggested a walk in the park next to the hospital. Once we were by ourselves, she asked if I had any questions about the previous night.

"How did you set something up so fast? It seems miraculous."

She laughed. "It certainly would've been if we had tried to do it in an hour or two. We started planning for a contingency like this the day she disappeared. Since her *friends* had threatened to murder her, I thought that there was a good chance something like this might occur.

"What happened to make this possible was that the brazen murder of Judge Adams and the attack on Elm Hill and Dr. Rydberg made some important people quite angry. Judge Adams was a personal friend of Governor Rutland, and the Governor used his good contacts with the Eisenhower administration to get the FBI involved. I don't know what technicality they used to justify it, but Dr. Rydberg was given an emergency contact number if anything suspicious came up. There was somebody ready to scoop her up."

"What will happen to her?"

"Well, I don't want even you or Clem to know specifics. Somebody, presumably with a sense of humor, decided to confine her in a mental hospital once they're done questioning her. In a few days, a uniformed policeman and policewoman will bring her into a psychiatric ward in a large hospital in a city such as Chicago or St. Louis. A psychiatrist will interview the police and examine Nora. A few days later, she'll commit her to a state hospital for paranoid schizophrenia. Then, after a year or two, she'll be released and go through Nursing School again to start her career over under her new name."

Chapter 13 ~ Who's a Duplicitous Doc?

Miss Mason, Detectives Perkins and Kempton, Mrs. Holdstrom, Laura, and I gathered in the administrative suite's conference room a few minutes before three on Monday. Mrs. Holdstrom and Laura had stenographer pads and several sharpened pencils in front of them. Given the several large plates of Swedish pastries and two coffee urns that were on the table, a long meeting was clearly expected.

At almost exactly three, Dr. Rydberg entered the room, causing Miss Mason and me to stand up as we were required to do whenever a doctor walked into a room. I noted that this made Laura wince and her fiancé smirk. Dr. Rydberg was a tall, thin man in his early 60's with receding grayish hair and a generally humorous countenance. Today, however, he looked quite serious, although he gave us a welcoming smile.

"Thank you for coming to this meeting. I admit that I'm very disturbed by what happened last week. It certainly indicates that somebody is determined to grab control of the hospital by underhanded methods and that Miss Mason and I are at the top of the list of people whose heads are scheduled to roll. That's not a very good feeling. I've devoted the last third of my life to creating an excellent facility for the treatment of the mentally ill. I could walk off to retirement tomorrow and be financially secure, but I shudder to think about what would happen to Elm Hill if crooked businessmen and gangsters succeed in taking over the hospital to steal its state appropriations."

Detective Perkins spoke up.

"Unfortunately, we've just dug up conclusive evidence about a gangster connection. If you can stay after this meeting, I'll go over it with you and your staff."

"Thank you so much Detective. I have a four o'clock meeting scheduled, but I can't think of anything more important than this for what I should be thinking about and doing.

"In any event, the time has come to discuss possible suspects inside the hospital. I really didn't believe that a doctor who isn't on the fulltime staff could aspire to be the new director as appeared to be the case in

June. Also, none of our staff who were arrested held responsible positions. I think that it's time to consider the senior staff."

Detective Perkins responded, "I think that it's really valuable that you agreed to meet with us. The police obviously don't have any idea about what goes on at Elm Hill, so any ideas you have about what should be investigated are more than welcome."

"I think that it's almost certain that one of our permanent staff is a major figure in this conspiracy. In addition to myself, there are five fulltime psychiatrists at Elm Hill. I think that we can eliminate Dr. Rita Harvey. It's almost inconceivable that any of the other Doctors would accept her as Director for two reasons. First, they probably look down on her because she's a woman. Second, her approach to psychiatry is much different from the way most of the people here practice. Consequently, it would not work very well if she were put in charge of the institution. There's another one who would be a long shot, too. That's Dr. Sam Rollins. He's only been here since January and came to us from Philadelphia. He's young and enthusiastic and is talking up the revolutionary potential of new drugs that are being developed and tested on the East Coast. None of those things endears him to his elders who perceive themselves to be his betters. There's one possibility, however, that you could check out. If he has some connection to the mob in Philly, they might have put him in touch with the Griggs gang and their corrupt business friends here."

"I doubt that anyone I know has personal contacts in the Philadelphia Police. In addition, we found out in June that the Griggs gang was looking to Chicago for mob contacts. Still, it never hurts to make a phone call."

"On the other end of the scale of likelihood is a name with which you should be familiar, Dr. Lawrence Carson. He's Elm Hill's Associate Director, who's in his mid-50s and young enough to take over the Directorship if I leave in the next few years. He would fire Miss Mason, if he had the chance, for being uppity. He certainly has substantial motivation. He also was suspicious during the treatment of Carrie Adams. His supposedly forged signatures were on several forms that ordered an unjustifiably onerous treatment of the girl. He either was grossly inattentive, which is certainly possible, or he was smart enough to give himself an out if the plan fell apart. Miss Mason, what do you think?"

"As you suggest, sir, I may not be the most unbiased person to give an evaluation of Dr. Carson. From what I see, he doesn't spend that much time with his patients, so it's possible that he could've just been ignorant of how Carrie was being treated. From what I know, he's competent in his administrative work. Also, he's in charge of the Electro-shock Theatre. At least some nurses think that's made him see patients as bodies, not persons. My impression is that he's also more likely than other doctors to prescribe straitjacketing and packing. If you don't know, detectives, packing involves wrapping a patient's body in cold wet sheets and leaving them totally immobilized for prolonged periods of time. He's not a nice person, but really, I've seen nothing to suggest that he's corrupt."

"Thank you, Dr. Rydberg and Miss Mason. I'll send Laura and Bridget Devlin, out of uniform, to see what their neighbors and acquaintances have to say about them over the next few days. They both look cute and innocent and have proven adept at getting lips to wag."

This candor made Laura blush. "Well, maybe I should be careful around Officer Sanders. Second, on our list of possible conspirators is Dr. Michael Sessions. He's in his late thirties and reeks of ambition. He's a lifetime resident of Osloville who went to State University for college and Medical School. He's been on staff here for the last ten years. He's a hard worker but seems to enjoy upstaging his colleagues. I haven't seen anything to suggest that he's particularly devious, but he could be sharp enough to keep that side of himself hidden. Miss Mason, what do you think?"

"The nurses have decidedly mixed feelings about him. He and Dr. Rollins impress us with how up-to-date they are on new treatments, so both are seen as good doctors. Yet, there's something about Dr. Sessions that sets nurses on edge. He's more obvious than most of the psychiatrists in his disdain for us. He's made it clear that he doesn't even want to hear our observations about patients and their treatments, and he probably pats more nurses' bottoms than any other doctor."

Detective Kempton guffawed, but it was Detective Perkins who spoke.

"Since he's a local boy, we should be able to check up on him. Perhaps he sat next to Ed Griggs in high school."

"Well, let's move on to Dr. Stewart Martin, the other member of our staff. The only suspicious thing about him is that he's far more arrogant than the other doctors, which makes him widely disliked at Elm Hill. He seems to do little more than go through the motions at work and is far more interested in the social life among the Osloville elite. Unless he's a lot deeper than anyone would give him credit for, I really don't think that he'd be interested in being Director."

"Still, we'll check him out. There aren't that many suspects among the doctors."

"Finally, concerning the doctors, I don't think that any of the ones who have practicing privileges here now are doing anything out of the ordinary. The one who might seem a little strange is Dr. Vincent Waller. He sent his daughter to Elm Hill to cure a drug addiction. Now, he's requested practicing privileges here to learn how to administer electroshocks. He's even sent a nurse from his clinic to work fulltime with Dr. Carson. Since Carson's involved that might be suspicious, but Waller has such a large practice at home that coming here even as Director would be a step down."

"Do you want us to check on him with the police in Springfield?"

"That doesn't strike me as a great idea. They'd probably be loyal to their hometown boy. That would just cause unnecessary bad feelings and alert people that we're checking up on Elm Hill's psychiatrists."

"What about senior nurses?"

"I've heard that you've arrested two nurses from the Violent Ward, including a charge nurse. Since that's the ward which is rumored to be at the center of the plot, you're off to a good start. However, it's hard to see either of the two in jail as being leaders in a plot. That certainly raises questions about the Nurse Manager June Rayburn. She felt that she should have been appointed Director of Nursing when Miss Lattimore retired. She feels that I made a horrible mistake in elevating her subordinate, Miss Mason, to that position and has manifested a barely concealed contempt for her. Consequently, she has a pretty strong motivation for wanting Miss Mason and me to be removed from the hospital. I think that several of the more traditional doctors would prefer her to Carol."

Miss Mason brought up another couple of somewhat contrasting points. "I agree that she resents both of us. Yet, she runs her ward quite effectively and hasn't challenged any hospital procedures or organizational changes. More particularly, she seemed at least a little miffed at Dr. Carson over Carrie's treatment and she was visibly upset by the way Nora manhandled Jane Greene last Wednesday."

"Well, especially coming from you, those views should caution us from becoming too suspicious. In addition, I don't know if it's worth putting too much effort into checking up on her. She lives in Brackman Hall, has a circle of friends among the older, more traditional nurses, and is an active member of the downtown Baptist Church.

"We should probably consider the nurse managers of the other nine wards. Three of them, Mary Thompson in Ward 4, Loretta Krebs in Ward 7, and Susan Wexler in Ward 10, are close friends of Nurse Rayburn. They're in the same generation, have the same values about the practice of nursing and patient care, and view Carol as an unqualified upstart. If Rayburn is involved in some plot, she probably has their support. If she isn't, on the other hand, I don't think that any of them are assertive or ambitious enough to get involved in a coup at Elm Hill. The other nurse managers were hired by Carol and seem to work well with her.

"Do you have any questions or observations, Detective Perkins?"

"No, sir. I think that you've given us more than enough to do and chew over."

"Great. In that case, please help yourself to coffee and pastries. I need to get away for about fifteen minutes to rearrange my schedule and see if any major problems have come up this afternoon."

Chapter 14 ~ Confronting Victor

When Dr. Rydberg returned, Laura gave him and Miss Mason a thin file folder.

"Here's a copy of a document that Richard would like you to have. When I went home yesterday evening, Mom gave me a manila envelope that, she said, a uniformed policewoman had delivered. I couldn't image what it might be, so I rushed into the living room and opened it. I was almost shocked to see that it was a four-page hand-written confession from Nora James. I called Richard and Matt immediately. Because of the suspicious circumstances in which I got the letter. They had me put on my rubber dish-washing gloves, hold the pages by the corner, and read the confession to them. As you'll see when you read your copies, she's pretty explicit about what she did and how the Griggs gang is up to something sinister in the hospital, but she really doesn't know what they're doing.

"Mom couldn't provide much more information about the messenger. She said that the woman who left the envelope was wearing a police uniform, but she thought it was a little different than mine. She also remembered that she was wearing leather gloves even though it's August. I didn't have my fingerprint kit with me, but Mom agreed to grasp a greasy glass to give us a good set of prints. The next day, Phil Dutton found that she, Nora, and I were the only ones to have left prints on the envelope or the confession, so we really don't have any idea about where it was written or how it got here. The only positive thing is that her nurse manager in Ward 2 said that she was pretty sure it was Nora's handwriting when I showed it to her earlier this afternoon.

"As you'll see, Nora was very explicit about Victor Buchanan's role in smuggling the pornography and drugs into Elm Hill. Detective Perkins had him dragged in for an interrogation at 8:00 this morning when he was still a little groggy. Why don't you read over Nora's confession, and then I'll play the interview for you."

"Thanks so much, Laura. This is starting to sound exciting. Have some coffee and a pastry while you wait."

The two read the four pages in about five minutes. I was pretty sure that Miss Mason had received her own copy from the mysterious "policewoman." Even if she hadn't, she knew what Nora had told us when she was at Clem's house. Still, she read carefully, presumably because she didn't want the detectives or Laura to suspect that we knew anything about Nora. By the time she had finished reading, she seemed pleased with the confession.

"I agree with you, Laura. Criminals are trying to do something to Elm Hill that's disgusting and frightening, but they evidently were smart enough not to tell stupid Nora anything about their broader scheme. Do you have any ideas?"

Detective Perkins replied. "No, unfortunately we don't have the slightest idea what those scumbags are up to. I can promise you, however, that Victor Buchanan is going to get far more police scrutiny than is good for him. Ed Griggs is one vicious gangster and won't appreciate one of his boys becoming a magnet for cops. Incidentally, he wouldn't let the patrolmen bring him down to headquarters until his lowlife lawyer, Manny "the Mouthpiece" Martin, showed up to accompany him. I don't think he wanted legal advice. Rather, he needed a witness to the Griggs gang that he wasn't squealing."

Laura then inserted a tape into the player, and we immediately heard the voice of Detective Perkins. "Mr. Buchanan, could you please tell us what your occupation is?"

"What business is that of the cops?"

"Your fingerprints link you to some criminal activity. We're trying to learn why you might have been involved."

"You don't have anything on me, or you would have dragged me down here in cuffs and thrown me in a jail cell. Should we blow this place, Manny?"

"Let's see what they want. We don't mind cooperating with the lawful authorities, even when they're picking on innocent victims. Just tell them that you're an entrepreneur, one of the people who make this city work."

"Yeah, detective. I'm a businessman. I buy and sell stuff. I do deals. It's not my fault that I make a better living than you do."

"Well, I guess you're a wise guy, Victor, but your business is certainly relevant to this interrogation. Your fingerprints were found on a several bottles of worthless pills that were smuggled into the Senile Dementia Ward at Elm Hill. How can you explain that? Do you own or work for a pharmacy? Or, do you distribute drugs for the Griggs gang?"

"I don't know anything about little bottles. Maybe I touched something in a bar or someplace, but I don't take drugs. You can test me, but you won't find anything. And how can you talk about the Griggs gang? That's just a fantasy of the lousy do-gooder publisher of the *Gazette*. Mr. Griggs is a reputable businessman. He's a major partner in Ernst Real Estate, Swedesborough Retailing, and Reynolds Construction. What are you jealous because he made something of himself?"

"Don't bluster, Victor. It doesn't become you. You're tied to those pills in another way. There were also fingerprints on it from Nora James, a nurse who worked on that ward."

"Never heard of her. Those girls in white don't turn me on."

"It's too bad you're not under oath, Victor, so we could send you off to the state prison for perjury. Our Vice Squad has been watching you, and you've been running around with a girl who looks like her. Some people even remember that her name was Nora. That's a little too much of a coincidence for me."

"Well, now you mention it, I did meet a chick named Nora at the Robbers' Roost a few times. Sorry that I didn't pick up on her right away. I'm a sexy guy. Lots of ladies like to be with me. Come to think of it, she did say that she was a nurse, but I don't remember if she mentioned Elm Hill. Maybe she was afraid that I'd think she was whacko for working with whackos."

"One thing that I'll give you, Victor, is that you've got a great sense of humor. If you ever go crazy, I'll tell the people at Downsville how to treat you. Getting back to the subject, however, what about the bottles that have both your prints on it? Do you remember handling it now? By the way, did you ever take her back to your apartment? Would we find her prints if we got a search warrant?"

"Put it this way, detective. We both like a good time. She's a hot item, so I certainly didn't mind being with her."

"You're a real romantic, Victor. I hope she appreciated your tenderness. But let's get back to the bottle of worthless pills. They weren't ones that the hospital got from its pharmaceutical company. She had to be bringing it in from someplace else. Since your fingerprints are on it, doesn't that mean that you gave it to her?"

"I told you I didn't. Maybe some stuff fell out of her purse, and I helped her put it back. If she took it into Elm Hill, she got it from somebody else. Why don't you ask her? Can't you keep track of one little nurse? You can't prove anything. Right, Manny?"

"They haven't said anything that a judge and jury wouldn't laugh out of court, Victor. Detectives, my client has never been in Elm Hill Hospital. If any crime has been committed, the nurse is the one who should be in a jail cell."

"That's a good analysis, Counselor, but don't you think that your client has a civic duty to put her where she belongs?"

"Hasn't he been cooperating? He hardly knows anything about her. She went to him for love and fun, not to plot crimes."

"Well, let's get back to Nora. When was the last time that you saw her?"

"A couple of weeks ago, I think."

"Well, from what I hear you've seen her since then. Does Tuesday, August 9th sound right?"

"Could be. What, were you, peeking in my bedroom?"

"No, that was the evening that Nora was caught trying to sneak back to her dormitory through a secret tunnel from the Muskrat River. What do you know about that?"

"All right. She had more spirits than were good for her and was afraid that she'd get in trouble if she staggered through the front gate. She said that she knew a secret way into the hospital. I agreed to take her to the entrance in a boat and get her boots and a slicker to cover up her nice clothes. I haven't seen or heard from her since. Did that nasty old head nurse stick her in a strait jacket?"

"You sound very chivalrous, Victor, letting a vulnerable young woman wander around in the dark and lonely place."

"She didn't worry at all. She had a big flashlight, and you don't expect people to be hanging out around a sewer drain."

"Did you ever go into the tunnels with her?"

"No. Why would I? We did all our business and pleasure in the Roost and my apartment."

"Well, Victor. I might believe you except for what happened next. After Nora got caught, she refused to say anything about what she was doing. They locked her up in their Violent Ward for the night to see if she might, on second thought, be willing to explain what she was doing to keep them from turning her over to us. During the night or early morning, somebody slipped her a note saying, 'If you squeal, you'll drown like a rat.' They also gave her a scalpel, which she used to attack a nurse and escape back through the tunnels. That sounds like you and the Griggs gang, if you ask me."

"If you keep insulting Mr. Griggs, Manny's going to sue you. Maybe he can make the city go bankrupt. That would teach you do-gooders."

"Well, that's something that I have to worry about, but let me give you something to worry about, too. Nora hasn't been seen since she scuttled into the tunnels last Wednesday on her way out of Elm Hill. A girl like that couldn't disappear on her own. Maybe you have her safe in a love nest, or maybe you took her fishing after putting her into concrete waders. If we can tie you to the murder of a poor little nurse, Victor, a guy like you will get the chair."

Laura turned off the tape and remarked that she wasn't playing Victor's not so fond goodbye because she thought that some of us might have sensitive ears. Miss Mason laughed.

"I also noticed that Richard was careful to give the impression that you didn't have any information about or from Nora. Her confession claims that she got the keys to the tunnel from Buchanan. There was another thing that you may not have the background to pick up on. When Victor bragged about the legitimate businesses with which Griggs is involved, he mentioned Reynolds Construction and Ernst Realtors. Nora's confession claimed that Buchanan told her that the Griggs gang found the tunnels when Elm Hill was being built. Clem worked on the construction and remembers that Reynolds Construction was the major contractor. In addition, the owner of Ernst is on the hospital's Board and is pushing to give the doctors who aren't on staff but have practicing privileges here more power over the administration. There's something rotten in Denmark."

Chapter 15 ~ A Strait Jacket for Sarah: Apprehension

As the meeting broke up, Miss Mason asked me to come back to her office at 6:30 after dinner. When I got there, I was a little surprised to see Laura and Officer Hastings sipping coffee with Miss Mason, both of them in their uniforms. I also noted that the two policewomen were wearing broad black leather belts with their guns and handcuffs attached. Miss Mason offered me a cup of coffee and a smile.

"Hi, Andy. Laura and I got a hunch after reading Nora's confession. We're bringing Nell, who's good at handling prisoners, to check it out this evening. If we turn out to be right, we'll need somebody to drive the hospital's ambulance. Normally, Clem would be the perfect person to come with us, but our target seems to have a thing about Negroes. Also, you're young enough to play the part that we need in our little scheme. Are you willing to help?"

"Of course, it sounds exciting. I noticed that Laura and Officer Hastings have their weapons handy. What's up?"

"Well, it's tenuous enough so I don't want to say anything right now. Enjoy your coffee, and we'll leave in a few minutes."

Laura then chimed in, "Your sister Jennifer got here last evening. My parents really like her. She spent the day with Rebecca Nordstrom, a meter maid, because I was tied up with sensitive stuff for the Elm Hill investigation. We'd like you to come to dinner tomorrow night. I'll pick you up at 5:30 if you'd like to."

"Thank you so much. I'd like to meet your parents, and I haven't seen Jennifer all summer."

After we finished our coffee, we went to the hospital garage, got the ambulance, and drove, mostly in silence, for about 25 minutes to the south side of town. Miss Mason had me drive down an alley behind a row of houses. I stopped behind a long, narrow house in the middle of the block. We got out and went up a concrete path to the back door, which Miss Mason opened with a key. I noticed that she was carrying a partially filled duffle bag. We entered a kitchen, turned on its lights, went a few paces down a hallway, and turned into a bedroom. Miss Mason flipped on a lamp by a bed while Laura then pulled the curtains closed and then walked toward the front of the house. Miss Mason offered a quick explanation to Officer Hastings and me.

"Laura and I got an inspiration after reading Nora's confession that another policewoman might be a very rotten apple, so we're setting a trap for her here. If she did what we suspect, we could get some very valuable information. She'll be sent here by her dispatcher in about 20 minutes. When she knocks on the door, Andy, please answer it and tell her that your mother and sister are in a back room. Then Nell and I will take it from there."

We waited in silence. I could see that Miss Mason looked fairly tense, which was rare for her. After close to half an hour, Laura called softly, "She's pulling up. It's her, thank heaven." I soon heard steps on the front porch and the doorbell. After Miss Mason nodded, I went to the door and opened it. A uniformed policewoman was there.

"Hello, you must be Sonny. Is your mother here? I'm supposed to see her."

"Yes, she and my sister are in the back. I'll take you there."

I turned and took a step back along the narrow hall when she grabbed my right arm, twisted it hard behind my back, snapped a handcuff on my wrist, pulled my left hand up next to it, and secured it. I must admit that her suddenness and strength shocked and completely subdued me, making my knees sag in humiliation. She grabbed the chain of the cuffs with one hand, reached back to shut the front door with the other, and hissed.

"You little pervert, diddling your own sister. I love to have a jerk like you in custody. Just wait and see what the bad boys at the jail will do to you. You certainly have it coming."

The bedroom door was open, and she propelled me through it, keeping a strong grip on the chain of the cuffs. I started to stumble forward, but then was jerked up as she stopped abruptly and gasped at the sight of Miss Mason and Officer Hastings whose hand was resting near the flap of her holster.

"Hello, Sarah. I'm glad you don't like incest. At least we can agree on that. However, Andy's my assistant, not an evildoer. Let go of his handcuffs. Andy, step away from her. I apologize for your treatment. I didn't realize she's so aggressive. Sarah, you certainly are living up to your reputation."

She released my cuffs, and I moved to the side of the room and turned back to see the policewoman looking puzzled and rather unhappy.

"What's going on? I have a good mind to arrest you all for filing a false police report. You better stay in your cuffs, young man, until I figure out whether I need to keep you as a prisoner. Nell, what the hell are you doing here? Are you involved in some plot?"

The policewoman's bluster was a complete failure. Officer Hastings sprang forward, grabbed both her hands, twisted her around, quickly handcuffed her, and finished off by using a second pair of cuffs to attach her wrist to her captive's chain. If anything, Sarah looked even more shocked and subdued than I felt when I had been similarly restrained.

Miss Mason responded in a soothing tone, "I apologize for the subterfuge. Really, we're trying to do you a favor by this surreptitious meeting. If we made a mistake, I hope you'll forgive us. We thought you might need to know that Nurse Nora was captured in Fargo this morning. She told the police there about her relationship with Victor Buchanan and about how she was met by a woman looking like you after her escape from the hospital. I'm sure, given your reputation, that you'll be included in an identity parade when she's brought back here in a few days. A lot of people think that you're a nasty bitch and would love to see you in a detention dress."

Officer Hastings turned Sarah around to face Miss Mason. Sarah clearly wasn't a poker player as surprise, fear, relief, and finally resignation played across her face. She certainly made no effort to disguise the fact that Miss Mason was right. "Well, at least that poor girl is safe. When I went back to the farmhouse where they were keeping her and found her gone, I was so afraid that they murdered her. Victor just laughed when I asked him later."

"Okay, Sarah. You've just admitted to participating in serious felonies. Do you want Nell's handcuffs or my strait jacket? The handcuffs might be more comfortable, but either the Griggs gang or their friends among the Guardians might want to make sure that you never get inside a courtroom."

I saw the policewoman's eyes dart downward to the duffle bag at the side of the bed, followed by a noticeable slump in her shoulders. "You're right. I could be killed if I'm arrested. I saw what you did to Carrie, so I know what you have to do."

"When we get to Elm Hill, we'll interview you. You'll never go to court, but there are too many dangerous things happening for us not to get all the information possible. If you don't cooperate, I'll send you to jail in the back of your own police car. Do you understand?"

"I don't have any choice, really, but I don't mind telling you everything I know. I certainly don't owe Victor Buchanan or the Guardians anything."

"Okay, Sarah. I'm glad you're cooperating. Long-term confinement in a psychiatric institution is a frightening prospect, but you've got yourself in so deep that the alternatives are probably worse. Now, it's hospital procedure to put all our straitjacketed patients in diapers. Nell, let's strip her from the waist. Thank you for being so docile, Sarah. You saw what we did with Carrie, so you should know that this won't be too bad."

Miss Mason kept her prisoner standing up, put on black rubber gloves that she pulled from the duffle back, gave Sarah a thorough rubdown of diaper cream, pinned a thick diaper tightly over her hips, and got her into a white locking rubber panty. Next, she had Sarah, once Miss Hastings had uncuffed her, slip on a hospital prison gown. Then it was time for the strait jacket. Miss Mason pulled the heavy canvas garment out of her duffle bag, made Sarah put her arms in the sleeves whose ends were sewn shut, turned her around and buckled the four straps on the back of the jacket. Finally, she showed Officer Hastings how to hold Sarah's elbows so that the patient's arms wouldn't be pulled too tightly together and buckled the straps at the end of the sleeves together behind Sarah's back.

After finishing with Sarah, Officer Hastings turned her attention to me and unlocked my cuffs. "Maybe you appreciate me a little more. That girl put them on so tightly that she must have hurt you."

"Yes, ma'am."

That made her laugh.

Miss Mason then called Laura from the front room where she'd been keeping watch and hurried us out the back door and into the ambulance to make sure that we were long gone before the dispatcher started to wonder what had happened to Sarah. The trip back to Elm Hill was uneventful. Laura sat beside me in the front of the ambulance while Miss Mason and Officer Hastings sat with their patient who was strapped to the pallet in the back. We drove in silence, perhaps because the presence of Sarah made conversation very awkward. As we stopped at a traffic light, Laura grabbed my hand, looked at me with gleaming eyes, and whispered, "We won."

After I parked the ambulance in the Elm Hill garage, an attendant helped us load Sarah into a wheelchair and strap her in. I thought we'd take her to the Violent Ward, but instead, Miss Mason led us to a small conference room at the back of the hospital on the first floor where she set up a tape machine. I helped the straitjacketed Sarah into one of the chairs. Laura then asked her to tell us about how and why she had helped Nora, but Sarah started telling a much longer story.

"I really didn't have any choice, but you need to understand why in order to know how I've been so stupid. I had a nasty childhood and became wild and rebellious. I'm sorry, Andy, that I was so rough with you, but my brother molested me. I still feel rage when I think of it. So, when the dispatcher said that a mother had notified social services about an abuse case, I really got juiced up and volunteered to go. How did you get her to say that?"

"Someone called in and said that she had just started working for social services and had this horrendous case. Since you're so enthused about arresting molesters, we were pretty sure that the dispatcher would send you without doing any checking. If someone else had shown up, I would have said that I had been called directly but found an unlocked house with nobody home."

"Well, you're a better planner and schemer than I am. In any event, I worked as a waitress for several years after high school in Julesburg where I grew up. Then I started seeing a truck driver whose routes covered the entire state. He told me that Osloville had hired a couple of policewomen and kidded me that their uniforms looked a lot sexier than my yellow waitress outfit. I rode up here with him, and we spent a heck of a weekend in the Playmore Motel in October 1948. I'm fairly athletic and knew how to use a handgun. So, much to my surprise, I was hired. The male cops looked down on us, but I fell in with the Guardians, a sort of secret society of crooked cops who work with the Griggs gang. They used me for sex, but I liked that. I also liked bossing the other policewomen around. I was really hardnosed, especially with prisoners, and got a pretty bad reputation.

"Please don't ask me for any information about the Guardians. They've killed several people who, they thought, might rat on them. If I'm seen as a possible threat to them, even being in here won't do me any good."

"Okay, I don't think anyone wants to take them on right now, but how did you get involved with the Griggs gang?"

"It was a New Year's Eve party this year. Sid Twist, the Vice cop, invited me to a party at the Roberts Hotel. I didn't have anything else to do so I went, even though he has a bad reputation. We went up to a suite on the fourth floor. Instead of a party, the only people there were the gangster Victor Buchanan and two prostitutes. We drank some champagne, and then the men started bedding us. Both of them liked rough and demeaning sex, so I felt more humiliated than turned on. Once they were satisfied, we took a rest. I was on a bed half asleep with the two other girls when the one who was wearing just her garter belt and nylons entwined herself with me. Before I could even understand what was happening, a huge flashbulb went off. Then Victor grabbed me by my hair and laughed harshly, 'You're my slave now, Sarah, unless you want to spend three years in Crawford for lesbianism. Just think what they'd do to a lesbo policewoman there!' After that he had me come to his apartment about once a month which, I guess, wasn't that bad. Sex was all he wanted.

"Then he called me at four in the morning last week. At first, I thought he just wanted me, but he soon explained that I had to help a stupid nurse escape from Elm Hill. I got one of my old dresses, picked up slickers and hip waders for us to wear, and keys to the tunnels from someone at the Robbers' Roost. I waded down from the little park on the up-river side of Elm Hill and made my way through the tunnels to the door leading to Elm Hill's basement. I had to wait several hours. Then

Nora came out in a rush. I took her to a farmhouse south of town that the Griggs gang had acquired. When I went back the next day to take her groceries and see how she was, she was pretty tense. I think that we both realized then, although we didn't say anything, that her future didn't look very bright. The second time I went back the house was empty. It had obviously been searched roughly, but the poor girl's toiletries were still there. Obviously, I thought the worst."

"Did either Victor or Nora give you any idea what she was doing for the Griggs gang."

"No, all I could gather was that she was a nurse and half frightened out of her wits."

Neither Miss Mason nor the two policewomen had any more questions. Laura quickly took her leave, reminding us that we shouldn't tell anyone else about her role in Sarah's capture. Once she had left, Miss Mason turned back to our new patient in a business-like manner.

"Thanks so much for being so cooperative, Sarah. Andy will take you down to the Violent Ward now. You can put her in Nora's old room. Once you get there, they'll get you out of your jacket and diaper. That should make you feel much better.

"Well, I think that we'll say that you're a paranoid schizophrenic who was seen by witnesses attacking a prisoner and that the city wanted you sent here as the quickest way to clean up their mess."

When we got to the nurses' station in the Violent Ward, I saw that Rachel had been replaced as charge nurse by Candy Rakowsky, a nurse in her late twenties who had been working with Rachel on the evening shift. I congratulated her promotion.

"Oh, Andy. Don't congratulate me. I want Rachel to come back so much. I'm so frightened for her. She'd never have anything to do with a slut like Nora. I can't believe that the stupid police could believe such a sweet girl would be involved with that stupid twit."

"I can't either. I know they have some evidence, but Rachel swears she's innocent. I believe her.

"This is Sarah Harker, who was brought here for paranoid schizophrenia. She'll be put in Nora's old room and go through Admissions tomorrow morning."

"Do you want me to get her settled in now?"

"No that's okay. I'll get her out of her jacket and tell her about ward procedures. Since I work on the morning shift which is the busiest, I think that I have a pretty good idea of what she'll be facing."

I got a pair of clean gloves at the nurses' station for handling Sarah's diapers. Once I wheeled her into the cell, she looked at me with a little fear in her eyes.

"Are you going to hurt me? I know I was rough with you."

"Heaven's no, Sarah. You're my patient. I feel sorry for you about how you got mixed up in such bad things without really meaning to."

On my way out, I found Officer Hastings waiting for me by the front door.

"Hi, Andy. What did you think of our evening's adventure?"

"You're really impressive, ma'am. I couldn't believe how you subdued the crooked policewoman."

"Well, she certainly got what she deserved."

Chapter 16 ~ New Issues

When I got to the Violent Ward the following morning, Mrs. Greene told me that Miss Mason and Miss Rayburn had assigned Sarah into my care and that, when Valerie went back to her regular ward in a little over a week, I would revert to three patients. Following breakfast, I escorted Sarah to the Admissions suite on the second floor and came back forty-five minutes later after the two Admissions nurses had finished processing her. Since nobody said anything about how to treat her, I kept her in the black-and-white striped gown that the criminally insane had to wear but didn't use restraints when she was out of her room in the Violent Ward. She was surprisingly subdued and said that Elm Hill was much better than the county jail.

The ward itself had certainly not returned to normal. We had almost double the number of normal packings. Two women became totally incoherent, gushing forth impassioned "word soups," and several ended up in restraints. Regarding my patients, given her notoriety, I kept Jenny in a strait jacket. Sarah stayed fairly inconspicuous. Valerie was so scared that she hardly left her room. Finally, Miss Delaware was one of the agitated women who were packed to calm them down.

When I went to the nurses' station after lunch to work on my notes, I saw that a letter in a hospital envelop had been delivered to me during the morning. I opened it with some interest and a little trepidation because I had never received an official missive before. The handwritten note inside was anything but official, however.

Dear Andy,

I love you. Nobody except my parents has ever done what you've done for me. However, your life is in College City and beyond. I hope mine will be at Elm Hill, but I'm afraid that I'm going to be sent to prison.

Please tell Miss Mason that Mrs. Greene started a nurses' war with me over treating a patient, Valerie Waller. I didn't understand it because it wasn't like her at all.

I'll remember you forever.

Love, Rachel

When I completed my nurse's notes shortly after one o'clock, which was later than usual because of all the activity during the morning, I went to Miss Mason's office and gave her Rachel's note. She looked increasingly serious as she read it and then tore the envelope into small pieces before dropping them into her wastebasket.

"Poor Rachel. I hope that you'll keep and treasure that note, but it might be a smart to make sure that nobody can trace it."

"How do you think it got here ma'am?"

"I have no idea, but it's certainly best not to inquire. Almost anyone here could have left it at a hospital mail drop. But how it got out of the jail is another question. I'm sure it didn't go out through official channels because they read all the inmates' mail."

"What are you going to do about her message?"

"Obviously, we need to get more information about the nurses' war between Rachel and Jane Greene."

"What's a nurses' war?"

"Every once in a while, two nurses get into a fight over how to treat a patient. Usually, it's between nurses on the same shift, but here it seems to be between the leaders of two different shifts. The loser can feel very humiliated and isolated from her shift, but gradually there's reconciliation between her and the other nurses because all of us know that we may lose out in such a dispute somewhere down the road."

"How can you find out what happened?

"That's what I've been mulling over. I don't want to ask people because that might raise some suspicion about what I really think is happening. The first step then is to review their nurse's notes. The problem there is that it would be unprecedented for me to ask Miss Rayburn for a copy. I don't think that there's any way to see Jane's notes. However, I've thought of an indirect strategy to see what Rachael had to say. I'll suggest to Laura that she get copies of Rachel's and Michelle's notes for the last two weeks, so we can go over them for clues about what they might have been up to. I know the police are still puzzled about why those two got involved in criminal activities. I won't tell Laura about Valerie, of course, because I don't want to get Rachel into any more trouble. I don't feel good about manipulating Laura, who's been so cooperative with us. Hopefully, she can find something incriminating in their notes to make it worth her while."

We then talked about Sarah briefly as we sipped coffee that was better than the usual brew at Elm Hill for some unknown reason.

"Well, Andy. How's our new patient?"

"I think she's settling in pretty well. She didn't get upset by either the wildness on the ward or the admissions process."

"Actually, I'm not surprised. Her life had really spun out of control. I think that she knew that she couldn't go on for much longer and ending up here is about as safe as she can be."

"Ma'am, I do have a question. You told me when I came to Elm Hill that half the cost for a patient is paid by the state but that the other half must be paid by her family. Who's going to pay Sarah's fees?"

"Ordinarily, that would be a problem. However, as I mentioned earlier, the FBI is quite interested in putting the Griggs gang and their crooked cop friends out of business. Sarah could be quite valuable to them, so they're going to take very good care of her. Don't breathe a word of this to anyone else."

That evening Laura and Jennifer picked me up in front of Brackman at 5:30 on their way home to dinner. Jennifer looked quite happy and gave me a hug as I approached the patrol car.

"Oh, Andy. It was so exciting today. Laura let me accompany her. She had to take four shoplifters to jail. There were so many of them that she and the store detective used all their handcuffs just to secure them wrist-to-wrist. One of the women was crying hysterically and another spat in Laura's face when she got them out of the car at the jail. But there's lots of drudgery in police work, too. The paperwork for those arrests took nearly an hour, and we had to sit around waiting for something to happen several times as well."

"Are you saying that you shoved all four into just half of Laura's back seat?"

"Oh, don't be silly. We had to use another car where all of the backseat is a lock-up."

On the way to the Sanders' home, the conversation was quite lively. Laura regaled us with stories of subduing and transporting unruly prisoners. I talked about my experience with strait jackets and packing.

Even Jennifer had an adventure to recount. Laura had lent her a pair of handcuffs for the week. On Monday, when she accompanied the meter maid Rebecca Nordstrom who didn't carry cuffs, she gave them to Becky who used them to secure an irate and drunken jaywalker to a handy parking meter until a patrolman could be called to haul him away.

The evening turned out to be quite enjoyable. The Sanders lived in a two-story frame house that was freshly painted and had a trim front yard, which made me think that Mr. Sanders was putting his retirement to good use on the home front. When I complimented them on their house, they looked pleased and said that it was fun working together. Mrs. Sanders also said that his retirement in 1952 was the happiest day in her life because she didn't have to worry whenever there was a knock on the door when he was on duty.

Mr. Sanders, like his wife Mildred, was in his late fifties. He looked like the stereotype of a policeman, stocky and muscular with short steel-gray hair. However, unlike the stereotype, he was cherry and affable rather than overbearing. His complex view of police work came out as he told Jennifer about how he felt about Laura's career.

"I was a cop for thirty years. I loved the job and am very proud of what I accomplished. I'm pretty sure that Mildred is proud of me, too. Some of the people on the force probably shouldn't be there, but we can't expect a perfect world. If men were angels, there wouldn't be any policemen. I was really pleased when Donny joined the force and Randy became a fireman. When Laura wanted to become a sworn officer after graduating from high school, I had mixed feelings. On the one hand, I was glad that she was following the family tradition. But the job isn't as good for a woman as for a man. Policemen must be tough and macho to survive, which I have to admit is not always appropriate. Policewomen don't get that much respect. Still, Laura is super enthusiastic, and, like Bridget Devlin, she's got family members and their friends to make sure that nobody does her dirt."

After an evening of easy conversation, Laura took me back to Brackman and exhibited her enthusiasm on the way. She certainly seemed excited about the meeting set up with her for the next day.

"I have a meeting with Miss Mason tomorrow at 10:30. She suggested that I get Michelle's and Rachel's nurse's notes and that we go over them together to see if we can find anything suspicious. The detectives think that both of them were probably mixed up with nasty doctors who led them astray. Do you think that we can find something incriminating in the nurse's notes?"

"I'm not sure. I know so little that all I do is describe my patients' behavior. For someone more sophisticated like them, however, you might be able to get an idea of whether they're paying extra attention to the patients of a particular doctor or doing something out of the ordinary. I think that you'd have to rely on Miss Mason for that."

"You're certainly right that I don't know anything about psychiatric patients. I have another idea, however. Could we see whether they were stealing drugs like Nora from their nurses' notes?"

"That's a good inspiration, Laura, but I don't think that you'd see it in a nurse's notes that would only report problems with medications. Presumably, if they were doing something illicit, they'd try to cover up any problems their patients would be having. I think you might be on to something, however. Nora might not have been the only nurse cooperating with the scheme. I think it would take a broader investigation. Why don't you ask Miss Mason about it tomorrow?"

Chapter 17 ~ Murder in the Mud

The predicted rain storm had settled in by the time I left for my seven o'clock shift the next morning. Fortunately, the storm outside was not replicated inside the Violent Ward. Our shift was fairly routine. I finished my nurse's notes about 12:45 and planned to do interviews for the next two hours because Miss Mason didn't have anything for me. I deposited the nurse's cap that I had to wear on the ward in my locker and headed out. I had walked about fifty feet down the dingy corridor toward the front of the basement when I heard a door behind me open and someone call my name. I stopped, turned around, and somewhat to my surprise saw Kathy Steele. She had always been polite but distant. Indeed, I couldn't think of any reason why she would need to flag me down.

"Hey, Andy. Someone left a note for you at the nurses' station. When I saw you going to your locker, I thought I should get it for you in case it's about something for this afternoon."

I walked back, and she handed it to me. As soon as she used her key to reenter the Violent Ward, I looked at it. My name was on the outside in printed letters. It didn't look like it came from either Miss Mason or Mrs. Holdstrom, which made me even more curious. I quickly opened it and got a shock.

> Andy,
> I need to see you immediately. Leave the hospital at 3:30 and walk toward the park. Make sure that you're in your full rainwear to make identifying you harder. Destroy this note immediately!

There was no signature, but I was sure that it came from Kathy. The park was in the back half of the four-block square hospital compound. Normally, there'd be staff relaxing in it during the afternoon and probably a supervised group of patients, but on a rainy dark day it would not be very attractive.

I turned left after I exited from Elm Hill's front door at 3:30. About halfway along the front of the hospital, a figure in black rainwear stepped out from beside one of the lofty elm trees for which the hospital was named and grabbed my right hand. I gave a little start, which drew a sharp whisper from her.

"The only reason that people would be going into the park on such a crummy day is because they don't have any place else to neck. Here, give me a kiss." I leaned into her. She was quite responsive.

"Well, Andy. We're both lonely, so that was nice. I'm pretty sure nobody has any idea who we are. I've been out here for ten minutes. I didn't see anyone paying any attention to me or to you when you came out of the hospital."

We reached the park in what seemed like just a few steps. Perhaps for security reasons, there was only one entrance on the corner across the drive from the hospital. Chest-high chain-link fences stretched away from the entrance to the high walls which surrounded Elm Hill that were a block away in each direction. The bottom half of the park, which we entered, was dotted with trees and picnic tables. Then came two rows of trees, hedges, and bushes in the middle of the park that marked the edges of what used to be an alley running the length of the block that was perpendicular to the hospital. On the other side of this, there were two tennis courts and several basketball nets. We started up a path that bisected the park diagonally. When we were about a third of the way to the old alley, Kathy stopped which meant that I had to since we were still holding hands.

"Andy, you must know a lot since you're Miss Mason's assistant."

"I don't know what you mean, Kathy. She certainly doesn't confide hospital secrets in me." I decided that I should be discrete, but her next question wasn't so easy to dodge.

"Who do you think I am?"

I hesitated for a moment before saying, "An agent for the FBI?"

This clearly was not what she had expected. She spun me toward her and grabbed both my arms just above the elbow with surprising force.

"What are you saying? That's so stupid! The FBI doesn't have women agents. Haven't the gossiping nurses and aides told you that I'm just a slut of a secretary who got caught by my doctor's wife and then was sent here because there's no place else for me?"

"No, ma'am. They don't gossip with me. I'm sorry if I made you mad."

Her grip loosened, but she still seemed upset.

"Oh, Lord. Why are you calling me ma'am? I'm just a lowly aide, like you. In fact, you're senior to me at Elm Hill. How can you think I'm a cop? Don't you remember how both of us were handcuffed and strip searched? Maybe you didn't hear, but they shackled me and locked me into a room in our Violent Ward for almost two hours. How could you think I'm tied into the police?"

"You're much too competent and self-possessed to be a girl who was sent away by her mother for disciplining."

I thought that this might enrage her which wouldn't have been all bad since it would have got me off the hook from answering her intrusive questions. Instead, she giggled, thanked me for the compliment, and then gave me an embrace and long kiss.

"Well, I guess that I shouldn't try to wheedle secrets out of you. In any event, we shouldn't stand here like we're having an argument in case somebody glances in as they're walking past the park. If we're so starved for affection that we'd go off in a rainstorm, we ought to be acting more lovey dovey."

She took my right hand again and walked me to a nearby picnic table. The benches were sopping with water, but our long rubber coats kept our bottoms dry when we sat on them.

"What I'm curious about is our new patient, Sarah Harker. I know she's an Osloville policewoman. The girls say that you brought her down to the ward Monday night, long after you were off duty. Is that true?"

"Yes, ma'am."

"If you want to neck in lovers' lane, stop calling me ma'am."

"What's lover's lane?"

"Don't you talk to the girls at all? See the old alley up ahead. Much of it is blocked off by trees, hedges, and shrubs. A nurse can go there if she wants privacy with a boyfriend, like an attendant, who's too cheap to take her to a hotel. Given my reputation as a loose lady that's one of the first things I got told when I got here.

"Anyway, let's get back to Sarah. Why was she committed here?"

"Miss Mason said that she had gone berserk and attacked a prisoner, but I don't know any of the details."

"What I'm wondering is whether she was connected to Nora's escapades and is now being warehoused here."

"Why don't you ask Miss Mason directly?"

"I can't have any contact with her at all since that could make some evil people suspicious."

"Aren't you asking questions around the Violent Ward that might make someone suspicious of you?"

"Heavens, no. I'm not so stupid as to make myself look nosey. Really, there are enough women raising questions about all sorts of things to keep me primed. I just listen to the gossip which can get pretty wild at times. I have some suspicions, but separating fact from fiction is quite a challenge."

"Have you found out anything that I should pass on to Miss Mason?"

"Well, now you're pumping me."

I blushed a little given the truth of Kathy's rebuke. "That's a good point. I really don't know anything more about Sarah Harker, but I can give you some information. I would guess that you know everything that was made public about the murder of Judge Adams. There were some things that didn't come out, however. Several shady businesses and the city's criminal Griggs gang were plotting to take over Elm Hill and then steal part of its state funding. One thing that they tried in June was planting drugs and pornography throughout the hospital to get honest people discredited and arrested. However, that plan fell apart on the night that Miss Mason and Detective Perkins tricked the murderer of Judge Adams into confessing. Then, Nora was involved with another scheme to smuggle contraband into Elm Hill, but after she was caught nobody tried to plant it within the hospital."

"We know that Reynolds Construction and the Griggs gang are deeply involved. After what happened in June, we got warrants for wiretapping their leaders. I don't know what we've picked up, but I'm sure it must be helpful."

"Ernst Realty also seems to be involved. Its owner is Bernard Ernst who is on the hospital's Board of Directors where he's trying to undermine Dr. Rydberg."

"Well, we got the strong impression that the Violent Ward is at the center of the plot. The people arrested in June were all too small fry to be leaders. I was supposed to keep a close eye on the doctors, the Nurse Manager, and the charge nurses. One thing that surprised me when I got here, however, was that the doctors, except for Dr. Harvey, have so little to do with the ward. I've been here over a month and am pretty observant, but I haven't seen any doctor do more on the ward than briefly visit a patient. If they're involved in something, it must be occurring someplace else."

"I don't think that Dr. Harvey's greater presence should be treated as particularly suspicious. It's a reflection of her different approach to treating psychiatric patients. Most of the doctors at Elm Hill believe in what's called medical therapy. According to my textbook on abnormal psychology, this assumes that a variety of mental illnesses, such as depression and schizophrenia, have physical causes that will respond to standard treatments, such as electro-shock. Once they make a diagnosis, they don't see much need for interacting with a patient. In sharp contrast, Dr. Harvey practices psychotherapy which assumes that mental illness stems from deep-seeded psychological factors that can only be uncovered by intense and prolonged individual therapies. Miss Mason calls Dr. Harvey a 'talker,' as opposed to the other doctors who are 'shockers.'"

"Well, you obviously know a lot more about psychology than I do, which really isn't surprising. Unfortunately, I haven't found out anything definitive about the nurses, either. Miss Rayburn obviously is resentful that Miss Mason was promoted over her to be Director of Nursing, but she strikes me as too traditional and moral to get involved with crooks. Among the charge nurses, I eliminated the two for the two swing shifts that service the ward. Jean Olson is a year from retirement, and Marcy Kurtz is young and inexperienced. Really, I thought the least likely one among the three who supervise permanent shifts was Rachel Weiss, but she's the one under lock and key now."

She got up, reached out, took my hand, and pulled me to my feet. We quickly reached the diagonal intersection of the path through the park with the alley. By mutual consent, we stopped, and Kathy's serious countenance was suddenly transformed by a mischievous smile.

"Well, we need to spend some time in lovers' lane in case somebody has been watching us. Take a couple of steps backward toward the hospital so we'll be hidden behind these huge bushes. There, you've been a good boy, so you get a kiss."

I reached down and pulled her tightly to me. Just as we had kissed long enough to start enjoying each other, my boot slipped in the mud of the alley, and I swung her around. When we broke apart, she started to giggle, which seemed a welcome departure from her strict character. Suddenly, however, she glanced over my shoulder down along the alley toward the far wall and grabbed my arms.

"Quick, Andy. Don't look. We need to get back on the path and out of here."

She was so commanding that I let her pull me back into the lower part of the park and then stood almost in shock while she ran down the outside of the alley toward the far wall, disappeared into some bushes about forty yards away, and then returned in less than a minute.

"Oh Lord, Andy. There's a dead body of a woman there. I think that she's been strangled because the ends of a scarf are coming out from under the back of her rain helmet."

"Do you know who it is?"

"No. Her back was to me. I couldn't see her face because of the helmet. I didn't want to disturb anything so all I did was check her pulse.

"Now, please. Listen to me closely. This morning, you asked me whether I'd like to get to know you better when we were milling around before Mrs. Greene's briefing. Then I suggested that we meet in the park at 3:30. Even though it was still raining, we decided to take a short walk since our rainwear would keep us dry. Please, don't tell a soul, not even Miss Mason or that policewoman friend of yours, what we talked about. I'm sure that I can trust you because if you were on the Griggs gang's payroll, I'd be the one dead in the mud."

"Yes, ma'am. You're much better at instant planning than I am."

"Oh, Lord. How many times do I have to tell you not to call me ma'am? If the wrong person hears that, we both will be in danger."

We ran, somewhat clumsily in our knee boots and raincoats, back to the hospital. When we got there, she had me wait outside the front door while she went in to call the police and tell Miss Mason about the murder. She returned sooner than I expected.

"The cops should be here within minutes. I'm sure we'll be separated, so remember what I told you. There's a nurse, Mary Terwilliger, who didn't show up for her 3 o'clock shift. Maybe she saw something she shouldn't have the night that Nora raised her ruckus."

I certainly was impressed with the agility of Kathy's mind. She turned out to be prophetic as we were placed in the back seats of separate cars when the patrolmen arrived.

Chapter 18 ~ Preliminary Investigation

After about forty-five minutes, Laura slid into the passenger's side of the front seat and looked back at me, somewhat balefully, through the wire mesh that separated the front and back of the car.

"I see they put you in a cage. Well, at least you're certainly not a suspect since you were on your shift at the time of the murder. Tell me what happened."

"Kathy and I made a date this morning to meet at the park at 3:30. We decided to take a walk to get better acquainted even though it was still raining. When we got to the alley, we stepped behind the hedge and started to kiss, but then she saw the body, pulled me back into the park, and went to investigate."

"Did you see the body? Can you tell me anything about it?"

"No, ma'am."

"Well, that takes care of our business, but I really don't like you getting involved with Kathy Steele. What do you know about her?"

"What do you mean?"

"Did you and Miss Mason listen in on our interviews of your shift after Nora's escape?"

"Yes, ma'am."

"Well, then you know. I'm almost in awe of what she's doing, but she certainly can't afford to love anyone. By all the way, you don't usually call me 'ma'am'. Are you a little embarrassed?"

My reply came out more sheepishly than I intended. "I guess so."

"Okay, let me get you out of there."

She got out of the car, opened my door, took my arms, gently pulled me up, and then led me to another police car where she repeated the process with Kathy.

With both women in their rain helmets, I couldn't see their faces, but Kathy must have looked surprised because she drew a response from Laura.

"Even though you're not handcuffed like our prisoners, I thought that I should help you out. Also, I didn't want you to get jealous if you saw the way I handled him."

I couldn't see Kathy's face, but I doubt that she appreciated Laura's ostensible solicitude. Laura then quickly turned business-like and changed the subject.

"Okay, you two. Thanks so much for your cooperation. I have to take you back to the park to make sure that it was your boots that made the tracks where you said you did."

We walked back to the park without saying anything. When we got to the point where the concrete path crossed the alley, first Kathy and then I inserted a foot into one of our previous boot marks. The results seemed to satisfy Laura.

"Don't worry about smearing the tracks. You lovebirds left more than enough of them, and Phil Dutton has already made plaster casts of the different tracks. It may seem silly having you come out here, but we need to dot all our i's and cross all our t's in case some sneaky defense attorney tries to say that our investigation wasn't complete.

"Kathy, you're free to go. It must be getting close to dinnertime. Andy, Miss Mason wants to see you."

Kathy interjected. "I need to talk with Miss Mason about my schedule. Is it okay if I see her for a moment before you two get down to business?"

"That's fine. She's in the garage at the back of the hospital where we've set up our situation center."

As we watched Kathy walk back down the path toward the park's entrance, Laura came up beside and briefly reached around my back and gave my right arm a pleasant squeeze.

"How are you? I'm sorry you've got involved in this. I must admit that I got a shock when I saw her, and she was pretty well wrapped up in her rainwear. This is the first time I've seen a murder victim. I'm glad you didn't actually see the body."

Laura's solicitude rather made me realize how horrible the crime was that had occurred.

"You just made me realize that this is probably worse for Elm Hill than the Adams' murder. We're supposed to provide a secure environment for our patients, but now it's hard to tell if anyone's safe."

"Are you scared?"

"I hadn't thought about it until right now. Maybe I should be."

"Well, I don't think that you have any dangerous knowledge, but you definitely need to be careful. Stay in public places as much as you can until we get the case solved. Maybe we should ask Miss Mason if there's a place you can stay in the hospital since your room in the basement is isolated. I'm sure that she and Dr. Rydberg are already thinking about how to beef up security."

"Well, I think that you're making me feel better."

"That makes me feel good. Kathy seems to be long gone. Let's go see Miss Mason."

As we approached the side door into the garage, we saw two figures in black rainwear standing under the awning outside the door. One came forward and took me by the arm. It was Kathy who spoke to Laura.

"Can I have a minute with Andy? Also, Officer Devlin wants to brief you about what's going on."

Laura responded with a somewhat unladylike grunt and walked over to the door. Kathy whispered good-bye.

"I've decided that it's time to leave. Bridget Devlin will walk me back to Brackman and help me pack. Then my contact will pick me up. It's too bad that we didn't have more time to get better acquainted. Now you can tell people about what we really did, by the way."

She then embraced me, gave me a long hard kiss, and called out to Laura.

"That should keep your fiancé from getting jealous."

Officer Devlin quickly came over to us and evidently decided that Kathy's quick departure was in everyone's best interest.

"Hi, Miss Steele. Let's get going while things are still chaotic so nobody will take any notice of us."

Then she came over to me, turned my helmet sideways, and whispered in my ear, "Just say 'ma'am' a lot."

When I reached her, Laura looked at me a little sharply but didn't seem to be particularly upset. I took the initiative but was quite deferential. "I'm sorry ma'am."

"That's all right. You obviously don't control her. I'm really curious, however, about what you were up to with her."

"I'll tell you, ma'am. Kathy just said good-bye to me so it can't hurt anything."

"Okay. Let's go over to that patrol car."

Once she deposited me in the back seat, I gave her a detailed description of our trip to the park and was rewarded with being lifted out of the cage far more gently than I had been thrust in.

"Well, I should've known you wouldn't be chasing a woman like that. Also, I'm pretty sure that you have someone who loves you and who's more appropriate and better for you."

"Oh, do you think that Helga's changed her mind about me? Why would she be more appropriate?"

"Oh, don't be silly. She's certainly not what you need. I know women who like to manhandle men. There are some policewomen, like Nell, who enjoy it. You deserve far better than that big hussy Helga. I warned her that if she tried to make eyes at you, Nurse Mason would deal with her. Evidently, I frightened her off, so maybe she's not such a bad girl after all. Anyway, nurses are like us. They're working class girls. They may be the salt of the earth, but they're not in the same world as college professors.

"Come on. Let's see Detective Perkins and Miss Mason before they send out a search party."

When we entered the garage, we saw Miss Mason and Detective Perkins deep in conversation at a table. Several patrolmen were drinking coffee and eating pastries with two nurses near the door going into the main building. We skirted around the ambulances and approached our superiors. Surprisingly, Laura addressed Miss Mason instead of Detective Perkins.

"Hello, ma'am. I know you must be thinking about increasing security after this terrible murder. I wonder whether you should move Andy to someplace that's less isolated and dark at night since everyone knows that he works closely with you."

This drew a smile from Miss Mason. "That's a great idea, Laura. I know that Dr. Rydberg has already ordered that people going to and from their shifts be organized in sizeable groups. I hadn't thought about Andy's being in the basement, but I think that you're absolutely right that he shouldn't be so alone. There's a murderer on the loose who's probably targeting people connected with the case. When we get done with our business, would you please escort Andy back to his room to get enough clothes to spend the next few nights in the hospital?

"I know that you've been tromping around the park for the last hour and that Andy has been sitting in a patrol car. Go help yourself to donuts and coffee by the door to the hospital. Also, there's a restroom over in that corner of the garage."

When we returned with our refreshments, Detective Perkins took over the briefing.

"The dead girl is Mary Terwilliger. The Medical Examiner says that she seems to have been strangled by the scarf that was found around her neck and that death probably occurred about midmorning. He'll probably be more definitive after he does the autopsy tomorrow.

"She and someone wearing attendants' boots entered the old alley at the same point that Andy and Kathy Steele did but turned in the opposite direction away from the hospital. They had walked side-by-side about half way to the outer wall when the attack took place. After the murder, the attacker continued along the alley and escaped through the door in the wall at the end. We've got several very good boot prints for him. I'm not sure if that'll be very helpful, however. Even though we can eliminate anyone who uses nurses' boots, most of the attendants presumably wore boots today, and probably more than a few have the right size. In addition, the killer could well have been an outsider since he left the hospital grounds. While we're checking all the boots we can find, I'm not very hopeful.

"Finally, let me play the interview that Miss Mason and Bridget had with Mary Terwilliger's roommate, Heather Stone, for Laura and Andy. After Miss Mason identified Mary, she came back to her office and called Heather in and told her about the tragedy. Bridget didn't even present herself to Heather until she had a chance to get herself together and be consoled in her grief by Miss Mason."

He then set up the recorder and popped a tape in.

"Hello, Miss Stone. I'm Officer Bridget Devlin. Please let me express my condolences for your loss. I can't imagine how it must be to loss a friend like this."

"Thank you, ma'am. Mary and I are close. We've roomed together for over two years and are really good friends."

"I'm sorry to bother you so soon, but we hope that you can help us find who committed this terrible crime."

"Yes, ma'am. I'll do anything I can to help you catch and punish him."

"What can you tell me about this morning? Did you see her? Was there anything abnormal that you noticed?"

"We both work the evening shift, so we normally have a late breakfast together. That's what we did today. We got to the cafeteria about 9 o'clock and stayed there about thirty-forty minutes. Most of the time we'd walk back to Brackman together, but today she said that she was meeting somebody. She was excited. I guessed that she might be starting to date somebody. She wouldn't tell me who it was, which was a little strange for her, but I assumed that she didn't want to get embarrassed in case it didn't work out.

"After breakfast, we went back to the big closet in the entry hall and got into our rainwear. She definitely was going outside the hospital for her meeting. She had one of her rubber boots fall off as she started to pull it on, which made her stop and giggle. Since I finished before she did, I kissed her on the cheek before she put her rain helmet on, wished her luck, and went on my way. I never saw her again. She was so happy, and that brute murdered her!"

She had sobbed a couple of times as she talked about their getting dressed for the outdoors, but her last sentence was conveyed with rage. Officer Devlin obviously felt the girl's distress as well.

"I'm so sorry, Heather. Do you want me to leave you with Miss Mason now?"

"No, please go on. If I know anything that could help, I want you to find out about it right away."

"What can you tell me about this meeting?"

"Not much, I'm afraid. I think somebody asked her during her shift yesterday. When we walked over to the hospital together at about 2:45, she was chatty. We work on different wards. I didn't see her again until we met a little after 11:00 to go back to Brackman. By then she was happy and excited. She said she was going to meet someone this morning but couldn't tell me who it was. That's why I thought that some man might be showing interest in her."

"Do you have any idea who it might have been?"

"I'm sorry, but I don't. It's probably some attendant, but I don't know why she'd hide his identity."

"What about a doctor? They got some girls in trouble in June, as you know. I get the impression that some of them are pretty bad to nurses."

"I wouldn't argue with you about that, but she's like me. We're not young enough or pretty enough to get a doctor hot."

"Was she dating anyone?"

"Not for the last few months. Also, I don't think that she would have hidden the identity of any of her past boyfriends."

"Was she wearing a red and blue scarf when you last saw her this morning?"

"No, I'm certain she wasn't wearing scarf, and I'm pretty certain that she doesn't have one that's red and blue."

"Do you remember the day that Nora escaped from the Violent Ward?"

"Of course, I do."

"Well, the detectives think that Mary may have seen something the night before that somebody involved with Nora thought was dangerous for them."

"I don't think so. I'm pretty sure that we came home and were in bed by 11:30."

"Could she have gotten up after you went to sleep."

"That's possible. I usually collapse once my shift is over. Mary has a weak bladder. She might have had to go to the bathroom, especially if she drank more coffee than usual. However, she didn't say anything or seem upset the next morning."

Once Detective Perkins had finished his tape, Miss Mason asked Laura and me to wait while she made a telephone call and went off to the little office in the right rear of the garage. While she was gone, the three of us walked over to the table by the door into the hospital to refill our coffee mugs and grab another donut. We had just sat down and had time for a sip or two of coffee when Miss Mason returned.

"I called Brackman Hall and talked to Emma Hughes and Bridget Devlin. Andy, I think that you can stay in the clinic that Emma runs with Dr. Harvey until we find the murderer. The clinic has two protected rooms and special security safeguards. Emma has the keys and has agreed to stay with you. Laura, if you'll escort Andy to Brackman, Emma and Bridget are waiting for you in his room."

Laura switched her gun from her purse to her belt, but the precaution was unnecessary as we saw nobody on our trip to the dorm. Indeed, there really wasn't anywhere for an attacker to lurk. The hospital's front parking lot was more brightly illuminated than normal which also provided lighting for the street down to Brackman, and a spotlight that had never been turned on before banished the usual darkness in the backyard and the steps down to the basement. The door to my room was open. It had two sets of rainwear draped over it and a small feminine suitcase, presumably Emma's, beside it. Inside, Emma was relaxed in my armchair, and Officer Devlin was sitting primly on my bed. Laura quickly gave us a shock.

"Hi, Bridget. Have you looked for the love letters from his naughty nurse and the pornography that you couldn't find in his locker?"

I saw a brief look of panic flash on Emma's face, but Bridget was evidently embarrassed by the question. Before she could say anything, Emma moved to divert the attention of the two policewomen as she would with an agitated patient.

"Laura, how can you say that about Rachel? Detective Perkins says that you have almost irrefutable proof that she was skulking about in the tunnels, but to claim that she seduced Andy and is having hanky-panky with some mysterious doctor is ridiculous. She's very religious and probably scared of men."

"I'm sorry. Please don't be mad at me, Emma. I was just trying to make a joke."

As the three women concentrated their attention on one another, I moved to my desk, surreptitiously slipped a small framed picture of my parents into my raincoat pocket, and picked up my psychology text, Bible, and a murder mystery, which I then dropped in a suitcase that I got from my closet. It took only a moment for me to add a pair of shoes, enough clothes for the next few days, and my toiletries to the suitcase. By the time I was done, the three young women were chatting happily about Laura's wedding next February.

When we got back to the hospital, the guard at the front door called Miss Mason and gave the two policewomen slippers to wear in the hospital. Emma and I put on the shoes that we had brought in our suitcases and showed our two companions where to put their boots and rainwear. By the time we finished, Miss Mason had appeared and promptly told us what to do.

"Hi. I'm glad you got there and back without any untoward incidents. Bridget, let me take you up to Ward 6 where Mary worked. I've talked with the charge nurse there, but it would be helpful if you questioned the other people on the shift about whether they noticed anything out of the ordinary about her yesterday. There's a good chance that she arranged her meeting while she was on duty.

"Emma, could you please take Andy and Laura up to your clinic and show them around? I'll meet you there after I've introduced Bridget to the people on duty in Ward 6."

Once she had unlocked the door to the outpatient clinic for abused women and children, Emma became a chipper tour guide.

"Originally, this was a reception ward for new patients. Two years ago, however, Dr. Rydberg decided that new patients should be integrated into a regular ward directly upon admission. Miss Mason had just become the Director of Nursing and knew that Dr. Harvey treated abused women and children in her private practice. She used the vacated space to start a larger clinic where she could get the help of several trained psychiatric nurses. Luckily for me, I was selected to be her part-time assistant. See, we come into a very nice reception area and waiting room. I love that brown sofa. It's so soft and relaxing. We want to put our patients at ease. We have some of the children's art work on the wall. That desk is for our part-time receptionist, Annie Tucker. Finally, look at the door. It locks of course, but we also have extra security with that heavy deadbolt. Miss Mason was worried that some abusive husband might be able to sneak into the hospital. In fact, several of our clients said that it makes them feel safer to have the door bolted behind them.

"Given the murder, Dr. Harvey felt that our patients might be scared coming to the hospital. Annie called those with appointments for Thursday and Friday, told them about the murder, and moved all the appointments to Dr. Harvey's private office on Cedar Street. We have sole use of this space until at least ten o'clock on Monday.

"Okay, let's go down this hall. Dr. Harvey has an office on that side, and my office is on this. The lounge doesn't get much use because we meet with our patients in the two meeting rooms that are over on the right. The bed over there, by the way, is the one that I use if someone's staying the night. If you need it, the restroom is off to the left. Andy, you'll notice that the two stalls have doors, unlike the ones for patients in the regular wards."

She then walked across the lounge and opened a door in the middle of the far wall.

"Andy, bring your suitcase along, and I'll show you the two rooms we have. They were designed to hold up to three patients, so they're much bigger than the ones in your Violent Ward. In extreme cases, when our clients feel physically threatened, we let them stay here, but we don't have any patients now."

We entered a narrow anteroom. It was about thirty feet wide and had two doors with observation windows like the Violent Ward. Laura jumped to the same conclusion that I did but giggled rather than cringed as I had.

"Oh, Emma. Are you going to lock him up?"

Emma blushed.

"That's our procedure for someone who needs protection. We don't want them wandering around and perhaps getting into trouble. Nobody's complained, and several of the ones who've stayed overnight say that it makes them feel safer. Here, Andy, let me unlock the door for you. Put your suitcase in there. You've got the choice of three beds. Also, there's a deadbolt on the door as well as an intercom that you can use for calling me in the lounge."

I quickly unpacked into a metal wardrobe and went back out to find Laura and Emma sitting with Miss Mason in the waiting room. I gave the outer door a quick glance and saw that it was bolted. Miss Mason gave me a quick smile, but her eyes remained serious.

"I see you gave the bolted door a glance. I think that we really have to be very careful now. The murderer had a key to the side gate, and there aren't many of those around. In addition, somebody who doesn't wish us well gave Nora keys to the tunnel and had keys to my office here in June.

"Let's move on to something more positive. Bridget and I talked with the charge nurse for this shift on Ward 6. She didn't notice anything unusual about Mary Terwilliger yesterday. She also doubts that either of the male attendants is involved since they're both in their sixties, never have been skirt chasers, and didn't seem to be very friendly with Mary. She said that the only other men who were on the ward yesterday, as far as she knows, were the attendant who ferried the meal carts for dinner and two visitors in the late afternoon. In addition, Mary escorted two patients to the offices of their psychiatrists, Dr. Carson and Dr. Martin, which also means that she could have seen any number of people when she was out of the ward."

This seemed to cheer Laura up.

"That's great news. At least we've now got some preliminary suspects and can get on to investigating them."

Just then the telephone on the receptionist's desk rang. Emma picked it up and called Miss Mason to the phone.

"Hello. Bridget? That's very good work. Give my best to Detective Perkins."

She then returned to her armchair.

"That was Bridget, as you must've heard. She found the nurse who sat next to Miss Terwilliger at dinner last night. She said that Mary was 'bubbling' throughout the meal, which wasn't characteristic of her. Unfortunately, however, that was after she would've seen all the men whom Charity mentioned. It doesn't help us narrow down the suspects."

Chapter 20 ~ A Strait Jacket for Sarah: Transportation

"Now, we've got another major piece of business for tonight. When Laura raised the possibility that Andy might be in danger, I had already thought about using the clinic to keep somebody safe, but that was Sarah Harker, not him. Incidentally, I've had Clem remove the dead bolt from the inside of the room where she'll be staying.

We need to get her up here. Here, Andy, is an order from Dr. Rydberg to have her prepared for transfer. Notice that it doesn't say where she's going. I'm hoping that people will assume that she's being sent to the Downsville Asylum. Bring her up the back staircase as if you were taking her to the garage. With all that's going on, I doubt whether anyone will remember for certain if a Downsville ambulance did or didn't pick up a patient. There's one other thing as well. If you can, put this scrap of paper between the door and its jam when Sarah is taken out of her cell and then check to see whether it's still there when you go on duty tomorrow morning. I'd like to see whether somebody tries to get in at night.

"Well, it's already a little after six. Why don't you three stop in the cafeteria before Andy gets Sarah?"

When I got to the Violent Ward, I found Candy Rakowsky, the acting charge nurse, at the nurses' station. She smiled at me more than a little wanly.

"Hello, Andy. What a horrible day. We haven't told the patients about the murder yet. Miss Rayburn and Mrs. Greene will go room-to-room after breakfast. All our staff are upset and frightened, so I'd guess that the patients can feel it. Most of them went to their rooms voluntarily after dinner. What brings you here so late?"

"Sarah Harker is being transferred. Miss Mason gave me this memo from Dr. Rydberg to prepare her for transport and take her upstairs."

"Gee, it's a little late to pick her up, but I guess that they can get her to Downsville for a late bedtime. Does she need to be sedated?"

"Miss Mason didn't say anything about that. At least when I've been taking care of her, she seems pretty tranquil."

"I think you're right, she hasn't caused any trouble on our shift."

Candy reached into the drawers under counter of the nurses' station and emerged with black rubber gloves and leather-padded handcuffs. When I looked at her a little quizzically, she explained.

"I'll have to get her heavily diapered because it will take at least three hours to get her transported to Downsville. I thought I'd toilet her in the staff restroom that's near her cell and handcuffing her should be enough restraint for that."

When we entered Sarah's cell, she was sitting on her bed. She looked frightened when she saw what Candy was carrying.

"Oh Lord. What are you going to do to me? And, Andy. Why are you here? Your shift was over hours ago."

Miss Rakowsky spoke to her in a quiet and reassuring way which let me know that she was a well-trained psychiatric nurse.

"Please don't be frightened, Sarah. Something awful happened in the hospital today which made Dr. Rydberg think that we can't guarantee your safety any longer. He wants to have you transferred to Downsville. Andy's here to take you to the Downsville staff because he's Miss Mason's special assistant. Do you understand?"

"Please, ma'am. What happened?"

"A nurse was murdered in the park next to the hospital, and everyone's afraid that our security can't protect us any longer."

Personally, I was very grateful that Candy had made the assumptions that Miss Mason hoped she would and was now telling a coherent story without my having to lie to her. I guessed that transferring patients to Downsville who were beyond the control of even our Violent Ward must be routine.

I waited while Miss Rakowsky cuffed Sarah's hands behind her back, pulled on her long black gloves, and took her to the restroom for toileting and diapering. When they returned, we got Sarah into her strait jacket and leg straps with no resistance. When Candy started to lead her from the room, I saw an opportunity to stay behind for a minute.

"Sarah, would you like me to bring the books that you have out?"

"Thank you. That's very thoughtful. Please bring the one that I was reading and the one with the green cover. I've finished the other two."

I got the two books, waited another thirty seconds, and then went to the cell door. The two women had already left the corridor and turned toward the nurses' station, so it was easy to insert the paper stub where Miss Mason wanted.

I caught up with them at the nurses' station. Since Sarah was wrapped up in her jacket, I added the books to the bag of her toiletries and took a strong grip on her canvas-covered arm. Candy walked us to the side door and let us out. I waited until we were well away from the Violent Ward with its many microphones before I stopped and explained to Sarah what the situation really was. Somewhat to my relief, she didn't appear particularly upset but pressed her upper body against me as a way of saying thank you.

When we reached the clinic, I rang the bell and Emma came to unbolt the door and took Sarah gently from me.

"Here, Sarah. Miss Mason has something to say to you and then I'll get you to your room and out of all that paraphernalia. By the way, I'm Miss Hughes."

"Thank you, ma'am."

We went into reception area where Emma sat Sarah on the sofa and then sat next to her. Sarah and Laura exchanged slightly strained "Hi's," and then Miss Mason explained the security setup in the clinic and why she thought Sarah needed to be here. Sarah's response implied that she was less worried about the threat to her than about what the move would mean for the conditions of her incarceration.

"After what you've said, I think that I feel safe here, but I do have one question. Will I have to be restrained like this because Miss Hughes is the only one here?"

Emma replied, "Well, I certainly won't keep you in a strait jacket, even when you're out of your room for exercise or toileting. I think that the leg straps are a good restraint to keep you from even thinking of running away. When you're out of your cell, in addition, I think that you should wear padded handcuffs. I'm well aware of what a tough lady you really are."

"Thank you, ma'am. That's fine. Really, I don't have any place to go."

Miss Mason used her last statement to segue into a new subject, an opportunity for Sarah.

"Don't be too sure about that Sarah. On Monday night you told us that you'd be afraid to testify against the Guardians or the Griggs gang. Well, those two ignoble organizations have got themselves on the radar of the FBI. The feds are willing to protect you and give you a new life in return for your testimony. Until the murder this morning, there was no hurry to talk with you about options, but now we seem to have lost control of the situation. Can you think it over and tell me what you want to do by Friday morning?"

"Yes, ma'am. It's scary to think about testifying, but it might be the only way I can have any kind of a life. I'll tell Emma what my decision is when on Friday."

"That's fine, Sarah. I do have two follow-up questions about our interview on Monday evening. Then you can get you settled in. First, do you know anything more about what the Griggs gang or the Guardians were trying to do with Elm Hill?"

"No. I'm sorry. I really don't have any idea. People like Sid Twist and Victor Buchanan use women as sex toys, but don't talk about their business in front of them."

"Finally, could you identify the prostitute who entrapped you for Buchanan?"

"They called her Mandy. She's looked like she was in her late twenties and was wearing a platinum blond wig. I probably could've gotten somebody in Vice to identify her, but I felt so dirty that I just wanted to forget everything."

This seemed to please Miss Mason.

"I think that's quite helpful, Sarah. Laura, do you think that you could get her identified? More importantly, if you do, could you put pressure on her to be helpful?"

"I'm sure that Lt. Simms who's in charge of Vice could find out who she is. He's good friends with Richard. Since Mandy helped to blackmail a police officer, I think we could make threats that are pretty credible to her. Those girls are scared of us."

She paused for a moment and then a mischievous look flashed across her face.

"Andy, would you like to be a decoy Saturday night instead of reading your psychology text and listening to the radio with Emma and Sarah?"

Miss Mason and Emma looked as puzzled as I felt, but a brief smile crossed Sarah's face.

"What's a decoy, Laura?"

"Usually, it's a woman who pretends to be a prostitute and decoys men into soliciting her so they can be arrested. About a year after I joined the force, for example, Susan Riston organized a half dozen of us policewomen into a decoy operation. Lt. Simms, Detective Perkins, and two patrolmen helped with the actual arrests. We filled two paddy wagons with tawdry men. Judge Lange, who's very conservative, loved us. Unfortunately, several of our prisoners turned out to be big shots, including a friend of the mayor and a church deacon. However, if we want to grab one of those 'working women' quickly, we'll need a man to pretend to be her customer. Those women can spot a cop a mile away."

"Can you give me more detailed information about what I'd have to do?"

"Well, we need to see if we can actually set something up. Then, we'll figure out exactly what we have to do."

After Emma had gotten Sarah safely locked up, Miss Mason still had one more surprise for me, which left me with somewhat mixed feelings.

"Andy, you've had a pretty distressing day. I'm a little concerned about how emotional you might become after the lights go out. It's still early but you have to be up at 6:15. I've got Dr. Rydberg's approval to sedate you for the night, and I'd really like to do it now unless you strongly object."

"Does that mean that you're going to give me a shot of chlorpromazine and then bundle me up in bed?"

"I can see you're worried about what you've seen in the Violent Ward. I'll give you a pill of a sedative that isn't as strong as what we use for out-of-control patients. Have you ever been sedated before?"

"No, ma'am. I guess that's why I'm worried."

"There's no need to worry, many of our patients ask for sedation at night. Since this is your first experience, however, you'll need to be put in a diaper and wear a safety harness which will give you much more freedom than bed restraints but keep you from falling out of bed.

"Emma, do you have what we need here?"

"I've got the harness and diapers that we have to use, but I'll have to get the sedative from Ward 4. I'll me go now. It should only take a minute. There are a few plastic cups in that cabinet over there. Andy, could you please get some water from the bathroom?"

When Emma returned, she gave her supplies to Miss Mason and unlocked the door to my room for her. Miss Mason then went out of her way to make me feel at ease.

"Don't feel nervous, Andy. This really isn't painful at all. The good news is that I won't need to shave you since this is just for one night."

My nod and smile must've looked a little forced because she immediately responded.

"Do you feel embarrassed that I'm treating you?"

"No, ma'am."

"Well, there's certainly no reason to be. Sedation is often good for people who've had a great shock."

She got me into my diapers and rubber pants and then picked up the safety harness which contained an intimidating array of black leather straps.

"Do you sleep on your back or your side?"

"I like to sleep on my side, ma'am."

"Well, for what we need to do that means that we can put your harness and gown on frontwards."

She slipped the harness over my head, had me put my arms under the shoulder straps, and completed the operation by pulling the pelvic strap between my legs. Once she put me into bed and administered the sedative, it wasn't too bad. I was pleased that my wrists and ankles weren't restrained and that I could roll around a bit.

She patted my shoulder and left with my instructions for the next morning.

"Goodnight, Andy. I'm sure that you'll sleep well. Also, there are two things that I want you to do while you're on duty tomorrow. I'll leave a note with Emma in case you're a little groggy when you wake up. Incidentally, Emma is going to stay in here with you tonight, so she can use the deadbolt. Laura has volunteered to stay in the outer room. She said that with a murderer on the loose in the hospital, it's a good idea to have someone here with a weapon."

I must admit that her references to being groggy in the morning and to the murder made me a little uneasy. As I was starting to conk out, I felt somebody sit down on the bed next to me and was too lazy to open my eyes. "Is that you, Emma? I'm definitely ready to sleep."

"No. It's Laura. Are you awake enough to talk for a minute?"

"I think so."

"I'm sorry that I was bitchy. That Kathy Steele really made me mad. Do you forgive me?"

"Of course, I do. We're friends. I'm touched that you're willing to stay here to protect us. You really are my guardian angel."

Chapter 21 ~ The Nurses' War

I certainly slept soundly and, as far as I can remember, dreamlessly until I was awakened by a hand shaking my shoulder and Emma's voice cheerfully admonishing me.

"Come on, Andy. Time to get up. It's already a few minutes after six o'clock."

I shook my head to clear the cobwebs and tried to sit up, but I was quickly halted by the fact that my bed harness was attached to a strap around the bed. This made Emma giggle, although she quickly apologized.

"I'm sorry, Andy. I shouldn't have laughed at you. Here, roll toward me. I'll unlock you from the bed strap. Now, sit up slowly."

I sat on the side of the bed with Emma holding my arm and felt entirely clear-headed, but Emma still pulled on black rubber gloves, helped me to my feet, and then gripped one of my arms firmly to lead me to the bathroom.

"Do you feel dizzy? I don't want to take any chances. Miss Mason said that she sedated you heavily. Don't feel embarrassed. After all, you get to see Laura and me in our robes, curlers, and hairnets."

After showering, I felt refreshed and wide awake. When I got back to my room, I dressed and opened the sealed letter that Miss Mason had left for me with Emma. It reminded me to check the door of Sarah's cell in the Violent Ward to see whether anybody had disturbed it during the night. It also asked me to try to find an opportunity for surreptitiously asking Valerie Waller about her treatment since she came to the Violent Ward, suggesting that I walk her through the storerooms' corridor because there weren't any microphones there. I had barely finished reading the letter when Emma came into my room, took the letter from me, and spoke to me briefly in a low voice that wouldn't have carried back to the lounge.

"Miss Mason told me to dispose of this. Also, I've moved your picture from your raincoat pocket to a locked drawer in my desk. We definitely can't let Laura see it."

Emma clearly was sneakier than I had thought. "How did you know the letter from Rachel was there?"

"If you want to be a psychiatric nurse, you have to be highly observant."

I got to the Violent Ward a few minutes before 6:45 and immediately went to the corridor with the staff restrooms and Nora's old room on it. As I anticipated, nobody else was around, and I quickly saw that the small piece of paper that had been between the door and the frame of the cell was now on the floor. I picked it up, made a quick trip to the restroom, and flushed it down the toilet. When I was going back past the nurses' station on my way to the kitchen for coffee and a couple of donuts, the door to the Nurse Manager's suite opened. Mrs. Wells and Mrs. Greene came out. The former gave me a hard look, but the latter seemed pleasant.

"Hi, Andy. Were you checking up on Miss Harker? Has she been acting up?"

"No, ma'am. Dr. Rydberg had her transferred last evening because he was concerned for her safety after the murder. I'm sure that Miss Rakowsky put the order in her file. The reason that I was there was to visit the restroom. Miss Mason sedated me last night, and that's made me quite sensitive about getting to the toilet.

"Would you like me to bring coffee and donuts for you and Mrs. Wells?"

"Thank you so much. Molly's just leaving, and I've already had coffee and donuts. So, go help yourself, but be sure to be back here in ten minutes for the staff meeting. Miss Rayburn will be there."

Mrs. Wells then reached for a blue pen that was on the counter but knocked it off. I retrieved it and handed it to her. She took it with no acknowledgement and then signed a document with her left hand. I hurried to the kitchen for refreshment, exchanged pleasantries with Robert and Velma Walters while I was there, and made sure that I was back at the nurses' station at seven for our Nurse Manager, who looked a little drawn.

"Thank you for being so prompt everybody. I'm sure this horrible murder is really going to agitate most of our patients. Mrs. Greene and I will visit each of them. After that, they should be individually escorted to the bathroom to clean up. I know that today is a showering day, but I think that we can postpone the showers to Saturday. They'll be fed in their rooms, and anyone who wants to exercise must be taken out of their room in restraints one at a time. Do you have any questions or concerns?"

Nobody did, but as the meeting broke up, Mrs. Greene pulled me aside.

"Hi, Andy. It's probably good that Sarah was transferred. You only have three patients again. Evidently, Valerie Waller has really been acting up. You'll need to use a strait jacket if she wants to go out of her cell, like you do with Jenny Sachs. It might not hurt to put a gag on her as well in case she goes berserk and starts her hysterical screaming. We'll need to keep her under strict supervision until she starts responding to her electro-shock."

This brought two thoughts immediately to my mind. First, the imposition of a gag reminded me of how Carrie Adams was gagged outside her room when she was first admitted to Elm Hill to keep her from communicating. Second, gagging Valerie would make it impossible to question her as Miss Mason wanted. I tried to get a little leeway in handling her by asking in what I hoped was a deferential manner whether I could have some discretion about her gag.

"The strait jacket should keep her secure, but could I remove her gag if she stays calm? I've found that talking with her makes her more tranquil. Really, she's generally pretty good for me."

"Well, I guess that's okay, but you should make sure that she's away from the rooms if you ungag her. Miss Rayburn will not be very happy with you if she starts howling and upsets the other patients even more than they are."

Since I wasn't involved in taking the patients to and from the bathrooms, I had time to relax and plan out Valerie's exercise period. Miss Delaware had told me when I woke her that she'd stay in her room because she hated being put in restraints. Jenny was toileted first, and Mrs. Walter brought her back to me in a strait jacket and rubber gag. I asked her if she minded her restraints. She just shrugged and, once Mrs. Walters had left, gave me a conspiratorial wink. Her parents were coming the following Monday, so she evidently wasn't going to let minor hassles disturb her.

I went to Valerie's cell and found her not very enthusiastic about exercising after being toileted in a strait jacket and gag. I convinced her to go, however, by telling her about the cover of the new *Saturday Evening Post* that had a rugged old lobsterman carrying a mermaid in a wooden cage on his back. This aroused her interest. So, we set off. We had a pleasant twenty minutes in the lounge going through the *Post* and *Look* and then wandered through the corridors for another ten minutes, ending up in the back hallway by the storerooms. I removed her gag, which clearly pleased her.

"Oh, Andy. Thank you for being so kind to me. Did you hear me giggle through my gag at that picture of the lobsterman and the mermaid? I'm starting to think that I'm like that mermaid, holding on to bars and not knowing where I'm being taken."

"I feel sorry for you, Valerie. What I don't understand is why you're being treated like this. Only Jenny Sachs, who stabbed her husband, and Carrie Adams, who was accused of murder, had such heavy restraints. You seem calm and under control, so there doesn't appear to be any justification for it. Have you attacked someone on another shift?"

"No, please believe me. Once I was brought here, I've been good. I admit that those nasty ladies on Ward 3 drove me out of control, but I haven't acted up at all since I was brought here and packed."

"How were you treated? Something must have happened."

"I came here exactly two weeks ago in the late afternoon. As I told you, Miss Weiss had Miss Rakowsky pack me. Once the sheets came off, Miss Weiss took me back to my cell and then brought my supper to me. When I stayed calm, she told me that I had to stay in my room for the rest of evening in case I became agitated again, but that I would be treated normally the next day if I didn't have a relapse. Friday was okay, but things changed drastically when I got up the next morning. Miss McClure woke me up and told me that the doctor had ordered restraints for me whenever I left my room. I knew that people get agitated and restrained regularly here, but I really felt humiliated when she took me to the bathroom and showers all strapped up. I stayed in my room all day and went to bed normally when the lights were turned off. However, sometime later, the charge nurse and a young attendant came in. Mrs. Wells told me that I had to be put in bed restraints and that she would supervise in case I wouldn't obey Miss Tuttle. Sunday was the same. I went to bed normally during the evening shift, but Miss Tuttle restrained me after she came on duty. I know that you looked surprised when you saw me Monday morning. Then, when Mrs. Bartholomew came to take me to the bathroom, she put me in a restraining belt and suggested that I stay in my room except for hydrotherapy. On Monday and Tuesday, I wasn't restrained during the evening shift. Once Miss Weiss was arrested on Wednesday, however, Miss Rakowsky imposed a strict regimen."

"That sounds pretty weird. Did you ever attack a staff member or lose control of yourself?"

"No. I've been docile ever since I got here."

Once I had finished exercising Valerie, I went to see Mrs. Greene. She said that with the ward under lockdown the women could handle the hydrotherapy, so I was free to go until lunchtime. I checked in with Mrs. Holdstrom who gave me two Swedish pastries and told me that Miss Mason wanted to meet me at 1:30 in the clinic. I then went up to the clinic and chatted with Emma for about half an hour. She told me that she had already had a session with Sarah about her childhood traumas and described the subterfuge that she had used to get Sarah breakfast.

"Laura stayed here until 8:30. I had the cafeteria bring up two breakfast trays, so the attendant who brought them would think it was for the two of us. Once she had gone, Laura went out to have breakfast with Matt, and I took a tray into Sarah."

"What do you know about a meeting with Miss Mason here this afternoon?"

"She wants to know if you were able to talk with Valerie Waller and to go over Rachel's notes about her nurses' war with Mrs. Greene over Valerie's treatment."

"I was able to talk with Valerie, and her treatment strikes me as a little strange, to say the least. I'm certainly interested in hearing what you and Miss Mason think about it."

Then Emma looked a little embarrassed and changed the conversation. "Andy, how have you felt today? Have you felt dizzy or confused? Many of my patients have had trouble with sedation when it starts until their body adjusts to it. Really, I'm a little nervous with you because you're my first male patient since Nursing School. I'm afraid that you may react differently from my women patients."

"Am I your patient?"

"Well, I guess you're considered an outpatient like the women and children in our clinic. Otherwise, how could I be treating you?"

"That's fine. You obviously know infinitely more about nursing and medicine than I do. Actually, it's touching how concerned you are for me."

Mrs. Holdstrom brought refreshments to our 1:30 meeting and then stayed to take down what was said on her steno pad. I reported what Valerie had said in as much detail as I could remember which drew an unhappy nod from Miss Mason.

"You're right that Valerie's treatment seems strange, but there's an explanation in Rachel's nurse's notes that I reviewed with Laura. Last Monday, when Rachel conferred with Jane Greene at the changeover between their shifts, Jane told her that Valerie had been diagnosed as suffering from hebephrenic schizophrenia and must be strongly restrained. Rachel checked Valerie's file and couldn't find any paperwork with such a diagnosis or order for restraints. She hadn't observed any behavior that would support such a diagnosis on the previous Friday, and Valerie appeared to be perfectly calm on Monday. Therefore, she did not have her restrained as Mrs. Greene demanded. On Tuesday, Rachel went through Valerie's file again and found no evidence of a recent diagnosis. Rachel, as you know, was arrested Wednesday morning so that we have no idea what happened after the end of her Tuesday shift.

"Andy, I doubt that you have a photographic memory of your Abnormal Psychiatry textbook, so let me give you a quick review of the symptoms for hebephrenic schizophrenia. It's linked to stress, frustrations, and family conflict which all apply to Valerie. However, the symptoms for such a diagnosis are another question altogether. The patient is emotionally indifferent and infantile and displays a disintegration of behavior and thought. She broods over fantasies, undergoes regression, and may act obscenely. Andy from what you say, Valerie seems fairly normal, which is often the case with girls committed here for 'being wild.' Have you even witnessed her, for example, being delusional, giggling inappropriately, or masturbating?"

"No, ma'am. That doesn't sound like her at all."

"I really didn't think so. Emma, do you have any comments."

"I haven't dealt with Valerie at all, but unless both Rachel and Andy have suddenly turned delusional, her treatment doesn't make any sense at all."

"I heartily agree. Gwen, would you please type up everything we've said. I want to give it to Dr. Rydberg well before he goes home so we can discuss it. Emma and Andy, would you please come by Gwen's office at 4:30 to get an update on what our next step is?"

I was a couple of minutes late when I went to Mrs. Holdstrom's office. Even though I had planned to be early, Dr. Rydberg's two secretaries, Denise Nuxhall and Carla Fischer, hailed me as I walked past to find out what I knew about the murder investigation, which wasn't very much. When I got to Mrs. Holdstrom's office both Miss Mason and Emma were already there. The latter's eyes were sparkling,

"Oh, Andy. I've got good news for you. Laura is bringing Jennifer to have supper with us. Your sister has a surprise for you."

Miss Mason smiled.

"I'm glad you have something to good to anticipate, Andy. I've some news for you as well, although I'm not sure whether you'll think the two items are good or bad. First, Lt. Simms in the Vice Squad has authorized you to be a decoy for the arrest of Mandy Chambers, the prostitute whom Sarah identified. Second, Dr. Rydberg decided, especially because of Mrs. Greene's odd behavior, that you shouldn't go back to the Violent Ward. Laura is worried about you, too, and thinks that you should stay in the clinic as much as possible.

"Dr. Rydberg is very concerned about the hullabaloo over Valerie Waller for two reasons. First, it's so nonsensical. Second, Bernard Ernst, the trouble-maker on the board, has just demanded that Valerie's father, who is working with Drs. Carson and Sessions on her case, be added to our board even though he isn't even a psychiatrist and lives three hours away from here. As a result, he's called for a meeting of the nurses involved tomorrow at nine in the administrative conference room. I'd like you three to listen in. Emma, I don't think you've ever been to our little *observation* room. I assume that you can find somebody you trust to stay with Sarah."

When Emma went to let Laura and Jennifer in she blindfolded me with a scarf. I heard some giggles and then the blindfold was removed to reveal Jennifer wearing a meter maid's uniform and black rubber knee boots that seemed clean and dry enough for the hospital. She was beaming. I guess that I must have looked shocked because there was another round of giggles from the young women before Jennifer offered an explanation.

"You really look surprised, Andy. Because meter maids aren't sworn officers, Laura got permission for me to be a temporary one to help Rebecca while she's working on the murder. I really felt good today doing something to help Osloville. Please, don't tell Mom and Dad."

Chapter 22 ~ Sorting Out the Nurses' Stories

I got up on Friday morning feeling much better. I had been able to sleep until 7:30, was especially pleased to have escaped sedation and a bed harness and was smiling at the memory of how excited Jennifer had been to be in a uniform. By the time I called them to unlock my room, Emma and Laura were dressed, curlers and hairnets put away, and giggling when I told them how pretty their hair-dos were. We had a nice breakfast and gossiped about what Dr. Rydberg's meeting with the nurses might turn up.

Mrs. Holdstrom got us settled in the small room whose door read "Janitor's Closet." It had a connection to a microphone in the Conference Room in the administrative suite. Emma looked surprised that this facility was available and then shyly asked if I had listened in to her interrogation by Detectives Perkins and Kempton in May. When I nodded yes, she blushed. Mrs. Holdstrom activated the microphone. There evidently were several people in the room as we heard shuffling and little noises but no conversation. At almost exactly nine, the door opened, and quite a few chairs were pushed back, presumably as nurses stood to honor a doctor.

"Hello, ladies."

"Hello, Dr. Rydberg."

"I've called you here because a dispute in the Violent Ward has just come to my attention. I want to interview you and bring a resolution to it this morning in view of all the problems that Elm Hill is currently facing. Denise is here to take notes so that we have an official record. I think that most of you know Officers Laura Sanders and Bridget Devlin of the Osloville Police. I've asked them to be here in case there's some connection of this issue to the police investigation. I don't think that's very likely, but we certainly need to be very careful in this environment.

"I'd like to start by conferring with Miss Rayburn and Miss Mason. Officer Sanders, please stay. Officer Devlin, would you please take the others out to the main reception area? I've asked Carla Fischer to make sure that there are enough chairs ready for everybody."

There was some general clatter has people left, but what was conspicuous was the lack of conversation. Once the door had closed, Dr. Rydberg became very serious.

"Good morning, Carol and June. I've called this gathering to discuss a nurses' war over Valerie Waller that just came to my attention yesterday. Ordinarily, I wouldn't have given it a second thought and probably wouldn't have been told about it in the first place. However, we're facing major problems. In addition to the murders, Bernard Ernst has just demanded that Mark Reynolds and Valerie's father Raymond be added to our Board of Trustees. I'm going to have to call in some political chits from the mayor and a couple of city councilmen to prove to some wavering Board members that I still have clout. I can also accuse Ernst, probably with some justification, of trying to take advantage of Judge Adams' death.

"June, it's your ward. What do you know about Miss Waller and her father?"

"Unfortunately, I don't know that much, sir. I've heard that her father was working with Dr. Sessions on her case, which several of us thought was a little strange. She was brought down just over two weeks ago on Thursday for a two-week confinement after she raised a real ruckus on her ward and in a seclusion room. She should've been returned to her ward yesterday, but I thought it better to keep her in the Violent Ward due to the chaos in the hospital and the deterioration in her condition.

"I don't know anything about a nurses' war. I've only had two communications about her. When I came to work on the Monday after her admission, there was a note from Marcy Kurtz, the charge nurse for the swing shift that was working in the morning over the weekend. She reported that her doctor had diagnosed Miss Waller as a hebephrenic schizophrenic who required strict supervision and restraint. Rachel Weiss had a special nurse's notes for Saturday when she wasn't on duty that raised some questions about what Marcy had said. After that, nobody referred it to me. I assumed that they had resolved their issue and that appropriate treatment was being provided because I didn't hear anything else special about Valerie after that."

"Thank you, June. So far things seem straightforward. Do you have anything to add Carol?"

"I hadn't heard anything about either Miss Waller's condition or a nurses' war until you contacted me yesterday afternoon. I did know that my assistant, Andy Russell, was taking care of her on the morning shift, so I asked him about her. He said that she had been treated normally on Friday. On the following Monday, however, he found her in bed restraints when he went to her room to wake her, and she's been in them since then. She hardly went out of her room during his shifts. I didn't know what her diagnosis was until just now, but I did ask him about whether she exhibited psychotic behavior. He hasn't had much training, of course, but he did say that she seemed calm and under control all the time that he was around her."

"Thank you, Carol. I'm still unclear about what's going on. June, could you please have your secretary bring up Valerie's file?"

"Certainly, I'm getting curious about her treatment myself."

"Denise, could you please call down to have Mary bring the file up to us? Then, ask Marcy Kurtz to come in. From what we know so far, she seems to be the one who initiated the change in treatment."

As Denise left the conference room, I whispered that perhaps Miss Mason had asked us to listen in so that we could get our stories straight. This brought a smile from Mrs. Holdstrom and a slight grimace from Emma who then patted my arm in consolation. We then heard the door in the conference room open, several chairs scrape, and Dr. Rydberg welcome the newcomer.

"Hello, Marcy. Do you know why we're having these meetings?"

"No, sir. I don't have any idea. It must be something about the Violent Ward since you've called in all the charge nurses and our nurse manager."

"We're just trying to figure out the treatment of Valerie Waller. What do you know about her and her treatment?"

"She's a patient who was assigned to the Violent Ward for a temporary two-week hold because she became uncontrollably psychotic on her regular ward and in seclusion. The first time I saw her was two Saturdays ago when we came on duty for the day shift. At our changeover meeting, Mrs. Wells, the charge nurse for the night shift, told me that Dr. Carson had filed a written diagnosis of Miss Waller as a hebephrenic schizophrenic and ordered restraints outside her room and bed restraints for her. I had Ginny McClure check her. Surprisingly, bed restraints hadn't been applied. We restrained her as required during our shift, and I passed on the order to Jean Olson, the charge nurse for the swing shift that followed us. Since then I've continued this treatment whenever our shift has been on duty."

"Thank you, Marcy. You said that Dr. Carson signed the diagnosis. I thought that Dr. Sessions was Miss Waller's psychiatrist."

"I'm sorry, but I really don't know anything about that, sir. She's scheduled for electro-shock. Dr. Carson administers shock therapy. Maybe he examined her and made the diagnosis."

"Do you know anything about a controversy on the ward over her diagnosis and treatment?"

"No, sir."

"Did you examine Dr. Carson's diagnosis?"

"No, sir. I didn't check Miss Waller's file. I leave my nurse's notes for Miss Rayburn. After she's done with them, she puts them in the file. Please, sir. I hope I haven't done anything wrong. I know that I'm young, but I really try hard and like my work."

"There's no problem, Marcy. You did exactly what you should have done. Don't worry about anything.

"Officer Sanders, would you please escort Miss Kurtz out of the administrative suite? Don't let her talk to any of the women who are waiting to be interviewed. Then bring in Mrs. Olson and see if Mary has brought up Valerie's folder."

This time it was Emma who broke our silence during the wait.

"I hope Laura doesn't jiggle her handcuffs at that girl. She sounded like she might faint."

This made us all suppress laughter since we weren't sure how soundproof the wall between our hidey hole and the conference room was.

Laura returned with a cheery note to her voice. "Here's Mrs. Olson, and here's the file for you, sir"

"Thank you, Laura. June, why don't you peruse the file while we're talking?

"Thank you for coming, Jean. There seems to be some controversy over the treatment of Valerie Waller. We need to talk with all the charge nurses. What do you know about the matter?"

"I know that Mrs. Wells and probably Mrs. Greene were having a nurses' war with Miss Weiss. Did they complain about me? Am I in trouble now that Rachel's been arrested? Is that why the policewoman is here?"

"There's no need to be frightened, Jean. I know that you've been a very good nurse for us for almost two decades. I can't image that you've done anything wrong. Now, please tell me what you know about Miss Waller's treatment."

"Yes, sir. My first contact with her was two Saturdays ago when we took over the evening shift for the weekend. At the changeover, Marcy Kurtz told me that she had been diagnosed as a hebephrenic schizophrenic who needed to be restrained for her own protection. Once she left, I checked Rachel Weiss's Friday nurse's notes for her because she keeps by far the most detailed descriptions of patients. I hadn't really thought anything about what Miss Kurtz had said, but Rachel's notes gave no indication at all of hebephrenic schizophrenia or any other serious psychotic disorder. I called Rachel at Brackman Hall, and she came right over because she really is very concerned about her patients. We interviewed Valerie together. She seemed normal and had no idea whatsoever why she had been strapped up to go to the toilets and then had to eat lunch in her cell during the morning shift. Rachel then checked Valerie's file and found no paperwork on the new diagnosis or order for restraints. We knew that Marcy is new on her job and concluded that she had misunderstood something. Saturday and Sunday I had Valerie escorted to and from the toilets and dinner, but we didn't apply restraints. By the time our swing shift returned to the Violent Ward, Rachel had been arrested, and Valerie was restrained outside her room and during the night."

"Thank you, Jean. I'm sure that you acted properly, so don't worry about getting in trouble. Do you remember what time Rachel examined Valerie's file?"

"It was a little after 4:30, sir."

"Did you examine the file yourself?"

"No, sir. She held the file and leafed through the contents."

"Did she remove anything from the file when you were with her?"

"No, sir."

"Do you think she had any other opportunity to access the file?"

"I doubt it sir. The files are kept in Mrs. Peters' office. As a charge nurse, Rachel has a key, but there's somebody at the nurses' station almost all the time. It's almost impossible to sneak in."

"Thank you, Jean. Don't worry about getting in trouble. Unless you've lied to me, I'll stand behind you one hundred percent.

"Officer Sanders, would you please escort Mrs. Olson out of the administrative suite? Then come back so we can discuss what we should do next."

Once Laura had returned, Dr. Rydberg tried to see if the group could make sense of what they'd heard.

"June, have you had a chance to go through Miss Waller's file? What does it tell us?"

"There's no diagnosis from Dr. Carson. We've been told that some of the charge nurses were in a nurses' war, but they clearly wanted to keep it to themselves. None of them complained to me, and the nurses' notes about Valerie don't say anything about a doctor's diagnosis. In skimming the notes, moreover, I don't find any reference to behavior that would be consistent with hebephrenic schizophrenia."

"That's certainly puzzling. Carol, what do you think?"

"Based on what we've heard thus far, I really don't know what to think. Why don't you interview Molly Wells next since she's the person who seems to have got the ball rolling?"

"I agree. Laura, would you please bring her in?"

Again, there was silence until Molly was seated.

"Hello, Molly. Thank you so much for participating in these meetings."

"Yes, Dr. Rydberg."

"There seems to be some controversy over the treatment of Valerie Waller. We're asking all the charge nurses on the Violent Ward to discuss what they know about her."

"She was brought in two weeks ago for a temporary confinement before being returned to Ward 3. When I came on duty the next night,

Friday, there was a manila envelope in my pigeonhole that contained her diagnosis as a hebephrenic schizophrenic and an accompanying order that she be restrained when she left her room and during the night for her own safety."

"Who signed those two documents?"

"Dr. Carson definitely signed the restraint order. I don't think that I looked at the signature on the diagnosis, but it was probably his."

"Okay. What did you do after you saw the diagnosis and order?"

"I put the documents into Miss Waller's file and passed the instructors on to Marcy Kurtz at our changeover meeting with the morning shift. About half an hour later, Ginny McClure came up to the cafeteria to tell me that Valerie hadn't been put in bed restraints on Friday night. I suspected that Dr. Carson might not have wanted to communicate with Rachel Weiss, the charge nurse on the evening shift, because she's too trusting of patients. We checked Valerie on Saturday night and found her unrestrained, so I had Lettie Tuttle diaper and strap her. This nonsense continued until Rachel was arrested the following Wednesday. That just shows what a disrespectful sneak she really is."

"Have either Dr. Carson or Dr. Sessions talked with you about Miss Waller?"

"Of course not, sir. You wouldn't see a doctor coming around the Violent Ward at midnight."

"You're right, Molly. I just wanted to check all the possible connections.

"Laura, would you please escort Mrs. Wells out and then come back in so we can discuss what we heard?"

Once Laura returned, Dr. Rydberg got right to the point.

"June, there's clearly bad blood between Molly and Rachel. Do you know what's behind it?"

"Well, they clearly have very different personalities. Rachel is intellectual and caring, while Molly is more traditional, like me. I think Molly may be a little jealous and rationalizes her feelings by saying Rachel is putting on airs. The big thing, I'm certain, is that Molly was truly shocked when she found out that Rachel is promiscuous when she caught her making love to Andy Russell."

Laura interjected herself into the conversation, quite forcefully at that. "That's preposterous, ma'am. We've got strong physical evidence linking Rachel to Nora's midnight escapade, but she's no harlot. Miss Mason examined her, and she's still a virgin. I've interrogated her several times and it's easy to tell that she doesn't know very much about men."

"Miss Sanders, you really seem to feel strongly about standing up for somebody whom you've put in a jail cell. I have no way of confirming or falsifying what Molly claims. Her husband left her for a much younger nurse five years ago, so perhaps that makes her suspicious of an attractive young woman like Rachel. In addition, despite Molly's innuendo, I'm pretty certain that Rachel has never had a major conflict with a doctor."

"Unlike me."

Miss Mason's aside was delivered in a cheerful voice, but it probably stunned Miss Rayburn, Laura, and Denise until she and Dr. Rydberg broke into hearty laughter after a moment's silence.

"Thanks, Carol, for breaking the tension. A little laughter never hurts. If you meant to suggest that Rachel's arrest and personal enmity between her and Molly are probably irrelevant, you've made a good point. Laura, have you heard anything that connects to your investigations?"

"No, sir. I'm sorry if I got hot under the collar, but I don't like to see even criminals accused falsely."

"I think that pointing out that Molly had got carried away was also a good point. Now, would you please bring in Mrs. Greene? Wait a minute, let's take a break. I know that Carla has coffee and sweet rolls out in the main office."

Emma and I took the opportunity to use the restroom, while Mrs. Holdstrom went back to her office in case Miss Mason needed her. We reassembled about fifteen minutes later as the next interview was starting.

"Hello, Jane. Thank you so much for meeting with us. We understand that you were involved in a nurses' war with Rachel Weiss over the treatment of Valerie Waller. Given Rachel's arrest and the recent problems on the Violent Ward, we need to make sure that this conflict wasn't connected to anything more sinister. Do you understand?"

"Yes, sir. I feel bad about it now, but I was only carrying out doctor's orders."

"I doubt that anyone's really to blame for anything here, Jane. Please just tell me what you know about the matter."

"Yes, sir. Miss Waller was admitted to the Violent Ward two weeks ago on Thursday by Rachel. Rachel is a very good and caring nurse, but sometimes she's just too lenient in treating out-of-control patients. After all, a patient isn't assigned to the Violent Ward unless she's prone to serious psychotic outbursts.

"Andy Russell was assigned to take care of Valerie during our shift. From what he reported, her packing on Thursday afternoon had seemingly got her back under control, so I didn't pay any special attention to her. When I came back on duty on Monday morning, I had a changeover meeting with Molly Wells whose shift had worked the weekend. Molly told me that she had received a written diagnosis of Valerie and a restraint order from Dr. Carson Friday evening. However, Rachel seemed to be meddling in things, causing Jean Olson's evening shift to ignore the order. I had Bertha individually escort Valerie to the toilets in a restraining belt and leg straps after Andy got her awake. At the changeover meeting with the evening shift, I gave Rachel a good piece of my mind. Then she got arrested on Wednesday. After that, everything was put right."

"Did you check on the paperwork?"

"No, sir. I submit my nurse's notes to Miss Rayburn, and she files them. I don't usually have any occasion to check the patient files."

Miss Rayburn said, "June, if you were so upset, why didn't you complain to me?"

"I'm sorry, ma'am. I would've if her defiance had gone on much longer. However, we really don't like to have our disagreements erupt into a major conflict because everyone looks bad."

"That's all right, Jane. I totally understand."

That essentially ended Mrs. Greene's interview, although a minute or so of small talk ensued. Then Laura escorted her out and brought Candy Rakowsky in.

"Hello, Candy. Thank you for coming in to talk with us. We understand that there was a nurses' war over the treatment of Valerie Waller and are trying to get to the bottom of what happened."

"Yes, sir."

"What do you know about Miss Waller's treatment?"

"She was hysterical when she was first brought in for a two-week confinement on a Thursday afternoon, so Rachel had me pack her. That seemed to calm her down. On Friday, I watched her closely, and she appeared to be tranquil.

On Monday when our shift came back on duty, Mrs. Greene, the charge nurse from the morning shift, verbally attacked Rachel at their changeover meeting for disobeying a doctor's order about Miss Waller. She threatened to report her to Miss Rayburn immediately if she didn't comply. Then on Wednesday, Nora escaped, and Rachel was arrested. Miss Mason saw me at lunch and informed me that I'd be replacing Rachel as charge nurse, at least temporarily. When I came on duty, there was a note in my pigeonhole saying that Miss Waller had been diagnosed as schizophrenic so that she needed to have a restraint protocol imposed. I went to see her and explain what we needed to do. She didn't seem surprised. I really thought that this was routine and didn't realize that there was any controversy. I hope that I did what was right and won't get in trouble."

"No, you're not in trouble, Candy. From what you say, you did exactly what you should have. Did Rachel talk to you about Miss Waller's treatment or about her disagreement with June Greene and Molly Wells?"

"No, sir. She didn't say anything about Valerie after I reported to her about monitoring Miss Waller on Friday. Although, several of us overheard her argument with Mrs. Greene on Monday."

"What was your relationship with Miss Weiss?"

"We're friends. I miss her. I really respect her, sir. She's so knowledgeable and always studying. I know I'll never be able to be like her. I really don't see how the police can think that she was involved with Nora Thomas. They lived in totally different worlds."

"Which world do you live in, Candy?"

"I'm sort of in between. I'm not a slut like Nora, but, unlike Rachel, I do drink, smoke, and date."

"Thank you, Candy. Does anyone else have anything to ask her?"

Miss Mason picked up the ball. "From what I hear, you're doing a great job, Candy. Miss Rayburn is very complimentary over how well you're running your shift under such trying circumstances. Don't worry about other people's fights. Just keep up the good work."

Dr. Rydberg then closed the interview and said, "I agree with Miss Rayburn and Miss Mason that you're doing a good job. Go and have a nice lunch and don't worry about hospital politics. Also, would you please ask Officer Devlin to come in on your way out?"

"Thank you, sir."

Officer Devlin came in almost immediately and said, "I hope you solved the problem, sir. I see that Laura didn't have to arrest anyone."

"Well, I guess that's good news. I'm more than a little troubled by the fact that documents seemed to emerge from and disappear into thin air. That's an unfortunate reminder of the problems that arose from forged doctors' signatures in May and June. I'll consult with Dr. Carson and Dr. Session and find out what diagnoses they made. Then, we'll do whatever they prescribe. In view of all the confusion, however, I'm suspending the electro-shock treatments for Valerie until I can review her records."

Chapter 23 ~ Decoy

I spent Friday afternoon and most of Saturday relaxing and talking to Emma and Sarah. They seemed to be getting along quite well. It struck me that Emma must have been one of the few people who had been kind and caring toward the disgraced policewoman. Miss Mason had joined us a little before seven when Officers Hastings and Prentice were going to pick me up to act as a decoy. I was excited but a little nervous about learning what I'd be doing.

The two policewomen were punctual and arrived wearing wide black belts with their weapons and handcuffs attached. Miss Mason asked what their plan for the evening was, and Officer Hastings laid it out.

"Mandy works from an apartment in an old house on 10th street. Her pimp usually hangs around in the lobby, but the detectives will arrest him right before we show up at eight. We'll then go up to her apartment on the second floor. Andy will go in. Alice and I will wait three minutes to make sure that he's given her the marked bills and arrest her for prostitution."

"How will you get in? Couldn't she destroy the evidence or hurt Andy if you bang on the door?"

"That's easy. We have a key. The landlord doesn't want to go to jail. We'll walk softly to the bedroom and then yell 'hands up.' Once she's in custody, we'll hustle her down the back stairs to the cellar which is connected to a garage that the landlord uses. There's a paddy wagon parked there. Once we get her into it, she'll be given two unpalatable choices. Hopefully, she'll cooperate."

Here, Emma asked a little tremulously, "What about Andy? Won't he run the risk of getting some awful disease from her?"

"He won't have time to do much. Most of our vice cops like to enjoy the girls, which I find disgusting. In any event, we'll give him a condom. By the time he gets that on, we'll have Mandy in handcuffs."

This made me more nervous, but Miss Mason and Emma seemed satisfied. Officer Prentice then continued. "On another part of the investigation, we finally got a chance to do some follow-up with Laura and Bridget on the three psychiatrists. I don't think that we found anything definitive, unfortunately. Just as Dr. Rydberg said, Dr. Martin looks like a long shot. He's pretty stuck up, but most of his attention is focused on socializing with the upper crust. Nobody we talked to thinks that he's very concerned with his job. The other two are much better fits for the frame. Dr. Carson is a bear of a man who seems to have a bear's appetite for food, drink, and women. His wife doesn't seem to mind, but she might not like the games he gets up to. Perhaps, he might need more money or want to be the hospital Director. Also, he seems to run in the same circles as several shady businessmen. Finally, we heard the most about Dr. Sessions. Almost nobody likes him, but most can't put the finger on what exactly bothers them. He's obviously ambitious and seen as using and discarding people, especially by his friends from before he went away to college and Medical School. He stayed away from unsavory kids back then, however, as he evidently saw himself as heading for a leading position in Osloville society."

The first part of our plan went perfectly, so I found myself being ushered into Mandy Chambers living room at a few minutes after eight. Mandy was short with striking red hair that cascaded down over her right shoulder and was wearing a lacy black negligee, dark stockings, and shiny black high heels. She certainly was quite sexy. She gave me a huge smile and ran a finger down the side of my face.

"Come in. You look nervous. Is this your first time or something? You've come to the right place. I know how to make you really happy."

She grasped my hand tenderly, running her finger up my wrist. I admit that I was excited as she guided me to her couch, sat me down, and gave me a quick kiss on the lips.

"Here, honey, get comfortable. Do you want a beer or a cigarette?'

"No, thank you."

"Well, you don't need anything to get you going. I take that as a compliment. Now, let's do our business, so we can start out enjoying ourselves."

I reached up and fondled her right breast, which drew a smile, and then gave her the two $10 bills that the policewomen had supplied. She walked across the room and put the money in the top drawer of a small desk. Then she came back, gave me another sexy kiss, and shepherded me back to the bedroom. Once we got there, she blew softly in my ear and then reached down and ran a finger up my calf. The effect was immediate.

"There, that should put you in the mood. Now, let's get unromantic for a minute. Do you want a condom? I prefer it because it protects both of us."

"Yes, please. I've brought one."

She took the condom from me and lubricated it while I sat on the bed and undressed. She was just pulling the condom on when the harsh voice of Officer Hastings made us both jump.

"Hands up. Both of you. Don't think your lousy pimp is going to help you, Mandy. He's already in jail."

Mandy bent down to me and whispered, "Be submissive or they'll really be nasty to us."

Officer Hastings was standing just inside the door with Officer Prentice just behind her. Both were wearing the rubber gloves that Emma had given them at the hospital for handling the prostitute. Officer Hastings moved forward, turned Mandy around and cuffed her.

"Well, with what you're wearing, you don't need much of a pat down."

Then she turned to me. "Okay, you don't need and pat down at all. Keep those hands up, stand up, and turn around slowly. You've obviously nothing to hide. Now, put on your shirt, stand behind her, and intertwine your arms with her."

Once I did what she ordered, she cuffed my arms forward through Mandy's.

"Did you pay her?"

"Yes, ma'am."

"Well, that's enough to convict both of you. What did she do with the money?"

My knees became unsteady at the prospect of being arrested. They hadn't said anything about arresting me.

"She put it in the top drawer of the table in the living room."

"That's a good boy. Now, you're calmed down enough so I can pull your pants up without giving you undeserved pleasure.

"Alice, I'll get the money on the way out. Do you want the front or back of our little train?"

"Let me handle the whore. Should we put panties on her?"

"They've got prison panties and bras at the jail. She doesn't strike me as someone who would get embarrassed by showing herself off."

The two policewomen giggled, but Mandy didn't seem to be particularly bothered.

Given the way Mandy and I were handcuffed together, we had to struggle going up and down the steps that we encountered. Our journey ended with three steps into the back of the paddy wagon. Once we were inside, Officer Hastings unlocked one of my cuffs, walked me to the front of the space, and attached them to the rail behind the bench that ran down the side of the van. Then she returned to the back, sat next to her colleague across from Mandy, and started questioning her.

"Mandy, we've already got his testimony and the marked bills, so you're definitely going to jail.

"What did you do to get him to cooperate? Why would he help you?

"We accosted him just before he knocked on your door and told him he was going to jail no matter what. However, if he helped us, he'd be charged with loitering and released with a fine tomorrow morning. I think he may have had some second thoughts when he got handcuffed, but it's a pretty good deal."

This sounded realistic enough to make me wonder for a moment where I was going to end up.

"You're another matter. What do you think Judge Lange will do when he sees your pretty face again tomorrow? Don't think that you'll get a lawyer or bail because your sleazy pimp is already in the slammer."

Mandy's face fell as she thought through the implications of the policewoman's terse threat. "Why did you set me up? I'm no worse than the other girls. Judge Lange will give me at least sixty days. He's so mean."

"You're not like the other girls, Mandy. You've messed with the Osloville Police, so you're on your way to Crawford State Prison. You know what they do to working girls like you there, don't you?"

"Oh, lordy. Yes ma'am. I'll have to service everyone. What did I do? Why are you doing this to me?"

"You set up one of our policewomen for Victor Buchanan to blackmail. Don't you remember your New Year's Eve party? She's just confessed. Now it's your turn to pay.

"What do you think will happen if we take you and your hot pants friend to the county jail and make sure that everyone knows that you're not there for turning tricks? Don't start to cry. Just answer me."

"I'll be killed before I can be questioned."

"Well, Mandy, you sound like a bright girl. Just like Victor told Sarah that she was his 'slave' then, you're my 'slave' now. Go ahead and have a little cry. I like to see hard cases break."

We sat in silence while Mandy sniffled and then composed herself. Officer Prentice pulled a Kleenex from her purse and wiped the prisoner's eyes and face after she had calmed down. Then, Officer Hastings continued in a much more sympathetic tone.

"I'm glad you're cooperating, Mandy. It's what's best for you. Knowing what Victor and Sid Twist do to women, I don't think that you'll lose any sleep about putting them behind bars for a good long time. It's lucky for you that the FBI has got the Guardians and the Griggs gang in their sights. You can help them, right?"

"Yes, ma'am."

After we parked in the garage behind the hospital, Officer Prentice came back from the driver's seat, guided her prisoner out of the paddy wagon, and escorted her toward the door into the main building, leaving me to Officer Hastings. She unsnapped my handcuff from the rail, but almost before I realized what was happening, she re-cuffed my hands behind my back and then cuffed me to her. This certainly stimulated my fears.

"If Mandy doesn't cooperate, will I have spent the night in jail?"

"I'm sorry, but if we have to arrest her, we'll need to take you in as well to make the prostitution charge stick. Don't worry too much. After we get you processed, we'll lock you in an interrogation room instead of sending you into the jail. Detective Perkins will than get you released in the morning and drop your arrest form into an obscure file. However, I don't think that you have to worry much about Mandy ending up in the local lockup.

"I'm a little sorry that we've had to treat you this way, Andy. However, you needed to look really upset when we took you and Mandy into custody, or she might have become suspicious. Come on, Miss Mason says we can listen in to her questioning in the little room that you've used to spy on us. She gave me the key and said that you can take me there."

Miss Mason had evidently instructed her about how to turn on the listening device, as she was able to quickly set it up. We then waited in silence for about five minutes before we heard the door open, people walk in, and chairs shuffle and squeak before an authoritative male voice started the interrogation.

"This is Agent Murray Ruskin. We are interviewing the prisoner, Miss Mandy Chambers. Also present, are Agent Thomas Downs, Officer Hilda Gardner, Detective Richard Perkins, Officer Alice Prentice, and Miss Carol Mason, the Director of Nursing at Elm Hill Psychiatric Hospital for Women. It's 9:18 on the night of Saturday, August 20th.

"Now, Mandy, have you signed a confession for aggravated prostitution and admitted to three previous arrests and convictions for prostitution?"

"Yes, sir."

"Do you know that this will result in six-months of incarceration at a facility outside this state?"

"Yes, sir."

A gruff female voice, presumably Officer Gardner, interjected.

"What about the little pervert who hired this streetwalker? Where's he?"

"Let's leave that to the local authorities, Hilda. They've turned over a valuable witness to us. Let's finish up here and be off before anyone who might object is any the wiser."

"Now, Mandy. Miss Mason is concerned about some goings on at Elm Hill and thinks that you might have pertinent information. We've agreed to let her ask a couple of questions in return for the local cooperation we've received in bringing you into our custody."

"Thank you so much, Agent Ruskin. Mandy, did you participate in a sex party on New Year's Eve with Victor Buchanan, Sid Twist, another prostitute named Cherry, and Policewoman Sarah Harker?"

"Yes, ma'am.

"Did you hear the men say anything about a scheme to take over Elm Hill?"

"Not then. They were just enjoying us. Starting in March, they mentioned Elm Hill a few times while I was servicing them. They wouldn't really talk business in front of us, but they laughed occasionally about how they were going to get rich by destroying the honest people at the hospital."

"Is there anything else you can tell us about Elm Hill?"

"Oh, yes, ma'am. Cherry and I were smuggled in for three sex parties in June and July. A nurse would pick us up, hide us in her trunk, get us into the hospital, and sneak us into the basement of the power plant. From there, we went down to an underground room that was set up as a bordello."

"Could you identify the nurse?"

"No, ma'am. She only came on rainy days when she could dress up in a slicker and rain helmet and kept her face covered with a scarf. She wasn't too tall, but I couldn't really tell how thin or stocky she was."

"What about her car?"

"It was a black two-door, late '40s Ford. I really don't know much about cars, and it didn't seem very distinctive to me."

"What about the entrance to the underground room. Where was it?"

"The back third of the basement is abandoned. There's such a maze of short corridors and rooms that I can't give you exact directions, but it's over toward the right side of the building. The trap door over the stairs going down is covered by loose plywood."

"Okay, what happened when you got to the underground room?"

"Victor and Sid came soon after us for their usual carousing. After an hour or so, they'd handcuff our hands behind our backs and put black hoods around our heads which had drawstrings that were pulled tightly around our necks. We were told that we'd be killed if the hoods came off. Then a third man came in and spent a long time playing with our bodies until he was satisfied."

"Can you think of anything that could identify him?"

"No ma'am. We stayed in our hoods until he was gone. When someone like Victor Buchanan threatens you, you know he means it. The two distinctive things about the mystery man aren't helpful unless you really know his private habits. First, he always took us from behind. Second, he's a transvestite who wore a soft nightgown or negligee, girdle, stockings, and heels to bed. I can still feel his rubber girdle and hard tummy pressing into me."

"Mandy thank you so much for cooperating with us. I have a very bad feeling about your mystery man. Good luck with putting your life back together. By the way, you'll be sharing the back of a police van with Sarah Harker all the way to O'Hare."

Officer Hastings switched off the intercom and gave me a reluctant smile. "Andy, I won't have to fingerprint, photograph, and strip search you, but you better wait here until that witch has gone. Do I need to take you to the bathroom or are you still okay?"

"I'm good in that department ma'am. Why did you and Officer Prentice run this?"

"There were two reasons. Now that nasty Sarah Harker is in a strait jacket, we're the two toughest policewomen around, and if Officers Sanders or Devlin had been involved, they'd have had to notify Officer Riston who probably would've made trouble.

"Were you upset about the handcuffs?"

"A little, ma'am, but I know that's the way you operate."

"You may have heard that I like to dominate men. When I was young, I had the same abuse as Sarah Harker. It didn't make me mean like her, but I like to see criminals in custody and won't get romantic unless I can control my boyfriend to keep him from abusing me like my father did."

"I can understand that. I'm so sorry for what happened to you."

"Well, you're fully restrained and got a reputation after smooching Kathy Steele."

She pulled me to my feet and twisted me into a strong embrace. We writhed against each other, making what I did with Kathy seem tame. Our rising passion was interrupted, however, when the door opened, followed by a gasp and an extended giggle from Officer Prentice.

"Oh, Nell. I see you're rewarding him for being a good boy. We really haven't been very nice to him for helping us tonight. Andy, I've got some more bad news, however. Miss Mason thinks that you should be sedated again."

Laura followed her a few minutes later, presumably to take me up to the clinic. The three policewomen chatted happily about their evening adventure, but I followed the conversation silently after all that had happened. Laura seemed startled by the others' description of my interactions with Mandy. Then she reached over and wiped the lower part of my face with a handkerchief before ending all conversation with the pronouncement, "Two shades of lipstick!"

Officers Prentice and Hastings quickly took their leave.

Once we were alone, Laura turned on me.

"What were you thinking of, kissing a dirty prostitute. I'll ask Emma if you need an injection. It may be worse with Nell Hastings. Do you like being handcuffed?"

"No, ma'am."

"Well, since you were in her custody, she's more to blame than you are."

We went by Miss Mason's on our way out and saw them relaxing over coffee and cookies. Miss Mason asked us to join them, filled our coffee cups, and passed us a plate of chocolate chip cookies. Laura took one and then handed me two more and bent close to whisper, "If you stay here much longer, you'll need a girdle, and I'll get you one. Men shouldn't have it easier than we do."

Detective Perkins asked Miss Mason what she thought of Mandy's confession.

"We've had a great day. The murderer's identity is clear now. Let's celebrate."

This drew blank looks from the rest of us, even Detective Perkins.

"Just think about what we've heard."

Miss Mason and Detective Perkins finished their coffee and rose to leave. She looked at Laura and me and gave us a parting jolt. "Richard has very kindly asked me to dinner at the Swedish restaurant on Main Street, but please don't tell anyone."

Chapter 24 ~ Catch, Release, Catch Almost All

When we returned to the clinic, Emma was excited to hear about the developments, although we didn't tell her about Miss Mason's date. She clearly wanted to talk.

"What are the new developments? I'll get some milk and cookies from the kitchen. It's not that late, and we can sleep as late as we want tomorrow."

We spent an enjoyable and companionable forty-five minutes chatting, although none of us could even guess what Miss Mason meant about the murderer's identity. Then there was a loud knock on the door, and Laura accompanied Emma to see who it was.

Emma returned holding something small wrapped in a white hand towel and looking perplexed. "It was a nurse I didn't recognize. Maybe, there's a swing shift on duty in Ward 4 tonight. Anyway, she gave me this and said it contained syringes with sedatives for you and Sarah. She even showed me a signed slip."

"Officer Prentice told me that I was going to be sedated, but isn't there a regular procedure for it?"

"Yes. I'm told to sedate a patient and then make the arrangements. Also, this is a much stronger sedative than you received before, although the pill worked fine. Also, Miss Mason must have known that Sarah is already gone."

"Emma, why don't you call Ward 4 to find out what's going on?"

"Okay, Andy. I'm really worried."

After the switchboard put her through, Emma quickly found out that the charge nurse didn't know anything about sedatives for Sarah and me and that nobody who even faintly resembled the nurse was working there that evening. This news agitated Laura as well.

"You need to contact Miss Mason immediately. She still should be at the Stockholm Inn. Someone could be trying to poison Andy."

Fortunately, when the switchboard connected us to the restaurant, Miss Mason was still there. "Hello, Miss Mason? It's a relief you're there.

Something strange and frightening has happened. About ten minutes ago, a strange nurse brought syringes with sedatives for Andy and Sarah and showed me a signed order from Dr. Rydberg. I called Charity in Ward 4, and she said that she didn't know anything about it."

"No, the nurse kept the slip with Dr. Rydberg's signature."

"No, she wasn't wearing gloves, but the syringe was all wrapped up."

"Oh, is that possible? Laura, do you think the nurse could have been a man?"

"I don't know, but Miss Mason is smarter than I am for thinking that right off after what Mandy told us what happened to her here."

"Yes, ma'am. I'll get Andy's sedation from Charity. After that, we won't let anyone in tonight and will look for an attendant with a signed note from you tomorrow."

We all slept late on Sunday morning and spent the day reading the Sunday newspapers and speculating about the case and some of the weird people involved in it. In the late afternoon, Emma got a call from Miss Mason who said that all three of us should come to the conference room a little before nine on Monday morning to witness an interrogation of a new suspect.

When we arrived at the conference room, it was already full. Detective Perkins was seated at the foot of the long table, flanked by Detective Kempton and Officer Devlin. The chair at the other end was vacant, a seemingly waiting hot seat. Miss Mason, who was sitting to the right of it, looked up, smiled broadly, and said, "Hi, there. I think that this will be a big surprise for you."

Laura moved to sit next to Officer Devlin, while Emma and I decided to sit on chairs by the wall behind Detective Perkins. The final person in the room was a pretty and serious-looking woman who was sitting across from Miss Mason.

Almost as soon as we were settled, there was a knock on the door, and Miss Mason called out in a neutral tone of voice, "Come in, Shelley."

My heart jumped. If Shelley were in trouble, maybe Rachel could be saved. The woman in brown quickly indicated that Shelley was in serious trouble. She got up as soon as the girl walked in, grabbed her by the shoulders, spun her around, and gave her a very thorough frisking, before putting her in a full set of shackles.

"Well, now you're ready for us. I'm Miss Carter. Don't even think of lying to the detectives. We know what you've done. If you can convince us that you weren't involved in the murder, I'll take you away to keep you safe until you can testify. If not, you'll stay here and end up getting your pretty hair shaved off when you go to the chair."

Then she pulled back the chair at the head of the table and lowered a stricken Shelley into it. I felt someone slipping into the seat beside me. It was Laura who was close to tears.

"Oh, Andy. I'm so sorry. I must have made a horrible mistake and got Rachel arrested. Oh, that poor girl."

I squeezed her hand in what I hoped was a comforting manner. Meanwhile, Shelley came out of her stupor. "Please, please, believe me. I couldn't hurt Mary. We were friends. I betrayed Rachel. I know I have to go to prison, but I couldn't hurt someone. I've been trained to help and comfort people."

Detective Perkins took over the interview. "Shelley, I sincerely hope that you can back that up. Now, tell us how you got involved in this illegal activity."

"Yes, sir. I was recruited in early March by Molly Wells, the charge nurse for the night shift on the Violent Ward. She said that there was a scheme to have some businessmen from the city take over the hospital, get rid of the current leaders, and siphon off the state appropriations. The people at the hospital who helped them could get promotions and payoffs. She knew that I was Rachel's roommate and was growing unhappy with the limited opportunities for promotion. She promised me a promotion to charge nurse and wanted me to keep an eye on Rachel and to tell her if Rachel tried to do anything to oppose them. I agreed because I didn't see how Rachel could be a threat to them. She certainly wouldn't get involved in anything dishonest, but she's so naïve and consumed with her job that she's oblivious to her hospital politics."

"What changed things. You framed her for your own crimes."

"When she first recruited me, Mrs. Wells took me to the Robbers' Roost, introduced me to the bartender, and told me that I should go there in case of an emergency. Then about a week before Nora was caught coming out of the tunnels, Mrs. Wells told me about the plot to smuggle pornography and drugs into the hospital to get Miss Mason arrested and Dr. Rydberg disgraced."

"What was the name of the barman?"

"He leered at me and said to call him 'Big Bad Bill.' He made me afraid."

"That's the one. You were right to be afraid of him. He's an enforcer for the Griggs gang."

The brown-suited woman broke in, using a much kindlier tone than when she had made the arrest. "See, Shelley, that's why you need to cooperate with us. We can keep you in protective custody. If you're not kept away from them, they'll probably murder you to keep you from breaking down under questioning."

"Yes, ma'am. I'll do whatever you want."

Detective Perkins then resumed his questioning.

"Tell us what happened on the night that Nora was captured. We know that you were in the Robbers' Roost about one a.m."

I gave Laura a look at this fabrication. She just smiled knowingly.

"Yes, sir. I was nervous that night because I knew that something dangerous was happening. I was still awake with my window open when I heard voices outside. I looked out and saw Miss Mason handcuffing Nora, who was wearing a slicker and hip boots. I immediately jumped to the conclusion that she had been caught smuggling the contraband through the tunnels. I couldn't think of any other reason why she'd be dressed in rainwear.

"I couldn't call Mrs. Wells because her night shift was already on duty. Then I thought that I could use Rachel's boots to make the police think that she was down in the tunnels, which would confuse their investigation, but my feet are too big to wear them. In any event, this was clearly an emergency, so I had to let the people at the Robbers' Roost know about it. Mrs. Wells had given me a key to the side gate. I got out of the hospital grounds that way and called a taxi to take me to the bar. When I got there, I went to the bartender who hustled me into a back room. About five minutes later, a short, dirty blonde came in. She said that I had done well, took the bag with Rachel's boots from me, and told me to be at the middle back door to Brackman at four. By that hour

Rachel was sound asleep, and nobody else would be around. I could get the boots back to her closet. I'm so sorry for Rachel. I never thought that the police would arrest her for a set of tracks."

"That's what we thought happened. What's missing, however, is any connection to Mary Terwilliger. Did she see you while you were sneaking around? Is that why she was killed?"

"Oh, Lord! I never thought about it. I did see her when I was leaving to go to the Robbers' Roost. She was heading into the bathroom, and we just waved at each other. She obviously didn't think anything of the encounter. When I saw her the next day, she didn't mention it at all."

"Did you tell anybody about this?"

"Yes, sir. The woman at the Robbers' Roost asked if I'd run into anyone who could recognize me on my way there."

"Well, from what we know, you really aren't linked to the murder. You need to go with Miss Carter now."

As we got up at the end of the meeting, Miss Mason walked back to us.

"Hi, Andy. I think you'll want to come with me on my next errand. Richard is going to release Rachel and Michelle. I'm going to pick them up and bring them back here. Emma, would you please make up two beds in the clinic. I think that we need to protect them until the murderer is under lock and key."

"Please, ma'am. Can I come with you? I need to apologize to those poor mistreated women."

"Certainly, Laura. I think that that might mean a lot to them."

"Ma'am, when did you discover that they were innocent? After their arrest, you told me that jail was the best place for them."

"I was certain that Rachel wasn't involved in any criminal activity. In addition, if she were being framed, Shelley would almost certainly have had to have been involved. I was less certain about Michelle, but I thought it probable that she had been set up as well. I told you that jail was the best place for them because it would keep them safe and not warn the plotters that we were on to them. I was also fairly certain that Molly was the woman who impersonated Helga. You may remember that Helga's bathing cap seemed to have been used by a left-handed person, and Molly and Rachel were the only lefties involved in the case. After Dr.

Rydberg investigated the nurses' war, in contrast, it became obvious that Molly and Jane were involved in something illicit. Thus, I was easily able to convince Richard that he should strike now."

When we got to the jail, Miss Mason said that I should go to the Visitor's Room, ask to see Rachel, and break the good news to her.

When I got to the women's jail in the basement, I was met by a young matron, who looked like she was just out of high school. She looked vaguely familiar. She saw my puzzled look and smiled at me as she ran her nightstick gently over my body.

"Mr. Russell, do you think I look familiar? I'm Emily Jenkins. We both go to the Lutheran Church on High Street. I sing in the choir. You signed in to visit Rachel Weiss. She's talked about you a lot. You're lucky that they let you come outside of regular visiting hours. You'll have this whole area to yourselves."

She left to get Rachel, as I sat down at a wide table that she had directed me to. After several minutes, the door to the cells opened, and I heard a gasp. Matron Jenkins led her to the table, sat her down across from me, took a handcuff from her belt, attached the back of Rachel's shackles to a ring on her chair, and stepped back 15 feet.

"Oh, Andy. I gasped because I thought you were my mom. She's the only one who comes to see me. I'm so glad to see you, but also I'm ashamed to have you see me like this."

"Rachel, Miss Mason brought me here give you wonderful news. The police are releasing you! They know you're not guilty now!"

It took almost an hour for Detective Perkins to get all the procedures and paperwork complete. The wait was more than worthwhile for the sight of Rachel and Miss Rice coming into the Visitors' Room in their regular clothes, a blue outfit for Rachel and her nurses' uniform for Miss Rice. Their eyes were red, but now they looked extraordinarily happy. Laura rushed up to them, hugged each nurse, and whispered to them for over a minute. Then the three women walked back to us and were greeted warmly by Miss Mason.

"Welcome home, Rachel and Michelle. I'm so sorry for what you had to go through. I knew from the testimony that first day who the guilty nurses were, but I didn't think that I could convince the police with my suppositions. More importantly, I feared for your safety if the plotters saw that the police weren't falling for their frame-ups. As we'll tell you in detail once we get back to Elm Hill, today will see the arrests of several nurses. However, the leader of the conspiracy in the hospital, who probably murdered an innocent nurse, hasn't been identified, so Officer Sanders is coming back with us to protect you until we can be sure that a murderer isn't skulking around the hospital. You'll stay in Dr. Harvey's clinic instead of your rooms at Brackman. Andy's staying there too. In fact, we just got tests results back today which show that somebody tried to poison him."

When we got back to the clinic, Rachel was overjoyed to see that her uniform had been brought over from Brackman Hall. Miss Mason smiled to see her obvious delight.

"I see you like getting your uniform back, Rachel."

"Oh yes, ma'am. As nurses say, our caps are our dignity. They show what we've accomplished and what our professional qualifications are."

"Are you a brave girl, Rachel? Would you like to go back to work today?"

"Oh, yes ma'am! What do you want me to do?"

"Jane Greene and Candy Rakowsky will be at the nurses' station before the start of the evening shift. I want you to walk up to them and say that you'll be the charge nurse for the shift. There's a microphone there, which is now turned on. Their reactions will be interesting."

Miss Mason accompanied Rachel when she left for the Violent Ward. Laura started to follow them, but Miss Mason stopped her.

"Stay here with Emma and Andy. We still have a murderer on the loose. Bridget has already made one arrest and has her handcuffs ready for this encounter."

"That's exciting. Who did she take into custody?"

"I'll let her tell the story when she finishes up down there. I'm sure that she'll enjoy telling it in person."

We had to wait nearly an hour on pins and needles before a beaming Bridget arrived.

"Well, I've really had a big day. When I got to work, Detective Perkins took me with him to put that mean Susan Riston under arrest. He told me that Miss Mason had told him this weekend that she was suspicious of how aggressive she had been when she came to Elm Hill.

So, he had her followed on Sunday and found out that she met with Nancy Brue, Victor Buchanan's gun moll, in an out-of-the-way restaurant last night. She's a real hard case. She just glowered when I got her chained up. Here's a tape of her interrogation. I really felt good seeing her in a detention dress and shackles."

We got our tape machine out, and she popped in a tape.

"We'll, Susan. You really are in trouble. You know what you'll get at Crawford? Both the guards and prisoners will hate and abuse you."

"Go to hell and take that fresh-faced little dope with you."

"Don't blame Bridget for your problems. She's honest and hardworking, not an embittered hag like you are. You were seen muttering with Nancy Brue in the Blue-Plate Diner for 40 minutes last night. I don't think that you were talking about inspiring Sunday sermons."

"You're a sarcastic son of a bitch, but it won't do you any good."

"Are you one of the Guardians?"

"Who are they? Don't tell me that you believe in the do-gooders empty rumors and title-tattle?"

"I'm glad that you don't believe in them. Then you won't be disappointed when they can't help you stay out of Crawford."

This evidently was the end of the interview.

"This afternoon was much better. I walked up toward the nurses' station with Miss Weiss. We passed several people who looked very surprised and mostly happy, but I put my finger to my lips to shush them. Miss Weiss was radiant. I think that she had probably forgotten the investigation and was overjoyed at going back to her normal life. As we walked up to the nurses' station, Miss Rakowsky and Mrs. Greene were deep in conversation. When we were about 30 feet away, Miss Rakowsky looked up, saw us, and seemed momentarily shocked. Let me play a tape of what happened next.

"Rachel! You're back. Oh, I'm so happy. I've missed you. The ward really needs you."

This joyous welcome was overwhelmed by a shriek of anger from Mrs. Greene.

"You interfering bitch! How dare you show your face here? We've had to save the ward from your gross incompetence, pampering of patients, and disobedience of doctors. Get out this hospital immediately! I'm going to see Miss Rayburn right now and demand your termination."

Here Officer Devlin broke in, sounding surprisingly powerful and in charge.

"No, you're not. I'm arresting you for participating in a criminal conspiracy to disrupt Elm Hill and steal state appropriations. In addition, you're under investigation for the murder of Mary Terwilliger. Now put your hands on your head, while I frisk and shackle you. You will see Miss Rayburn, but she'll be sitting in on your interrogation in her conference room."

Detective Perkins started the interview in a professional manner.

"Mrs. Green. We know that Miss Weiss is innocent. She was arrested because of planted evidence. Her roommate, Shelley Newton, has confessed to her part in framing Miss Weiss as part of a larger plot to plant contraband in Elm Hill to discredit the hospital's leadership. She has been taken into custody and will provide valuable evidence about what's been going on. Your only hope to avoid a long term in state prison is to cooperate.

"Since Miss Weiss is clearly innocent, your extreme reaction to seeing her and your unwarranted accusations against her mark you as a guilty party to this plot. If you're willing to cooperate the State's Attorney, who is represented here by Mr. Yost, is ready to offer you a two-year term in Crawford. Isn't that right sir?"

"Yes, it is. I'd advise you to take it, Jane. Just answer Detective Perkins' questions, and you'll still have time to regain your life afterwards."

Here, Detective Perkins took over again.

"How did you get involved in this, Jane."

"I was blackmailed in February by that psychopathic creature who was sent back to the tightest insane asylum in Chicago. She had me initial a drug order from Dr. Carson for four of his patients in the Violent Ward. I just glanced at it and signed it without thinking. Then she came back the next day with a wide smile and had me read the order closely. Dr. Carson's signature didn't look quite right. She said that my written initials were proof of forgery and that she would have me sent to prison for 15 years if I didn't do what she told me. However, she never said anything about it again.

"Then about a week before the Nora fiasco, Molly Wells confronted me when we were in the Nurse Manager's suite talking about a couple of problem patients. She showed me the note and said that I had to cooperate in planting contraband to discredit the hospital's administration and let 'real businessmen' run it properly. She didn't have anything specific for me to do but wanted me to be on my toes if I were needed.

"I didn't hear anything until the morning after Nora was caught. Then when I went to the street to get my car at 5:45, I was met by a short woman who was so bundled up that all I could see of her was her eyes. She told me what had happened with Nora, gave me the note and the scalpel, and told me the plan for Nora's escape. When I got to the Violent Ward at 6:15, I immediately went to Molly. Most of her shift were heading their lockers by the side exit, and it was still a little early for anyone on my shift to be arriving. Molly got the idea of incriminating Helga because of the distinctiveness of her blue bathing cap. She hustled out to get the cap and went to the dayroom to read, looking very innocent if anyone noticed her. Then when Robert went to check out the toilets after our staff meeting, she put on Helga's cap and her own protective wear, made sure that Robert noticed her as she was kneeling, went to Nora's room, exited through the lounge and dayroom, and went around the outside of the ward to put the cap back in Helga's locker."

Officer Devlin removed the tape with a satisfied smile.

Laura was curious about the implications of the confession.

"What's going to happen to Molly? I think she's really evil. She's a major reason that we were misled into arresting Rachel."

"She's probably in the same paddy wagon with Mrs. Greene. When I came up here, Miss Mason was taking Detective Perkins and Matron Rawlings up to her room to take her into custody and cart her off to the slammer."

Chapter 25 ~ Twisted

Officer Devlin also told us that we should go to a meeting with Detective Perkins in Miss Mason's office at four. When Laura and I arrived, the detective was beaming.

"I think that I have something that should be very interesting. When the name of Sid Twist of the Vice Squad came up in Mandy's confession, it sparked a bad memory. By the way, he's also called Twisted for the way he treats prostitutes. He was the cop who had told me that Emma was spying on the Violent Ward and trying to help Carrie Adams escape justice last May. Anyway, I went pounding on his door early this morning. As I expected, he was hung over and groggy, which made my job a little easier. I told him that I wanted some information from him to help with the Terwilliger case and that I would buy him breakfast at Sue's Corner. Since they have huge servings and decent food, he was interested enough to say yes. Since Sue owes me, she had given us a little room to ourselves and allowed me to set up a hidden recorder. I was hoping to lead him up to a credible threat without him realizing what was happening. I took a gamble and struck gold."

He popped a tape into the Miss Mason's player.

"Well, Sid. You don't look so chipper. Were you on duty last night?"

"Sure was. Any night has got lots of vice, so we need to be out."

"Were you playing with prostitutes? I doubt that you were hassling Victor Buchanan and his drug boys."

"What are you implying? We were just doing our job. We got five girls. Four of them ended up in the paddy wagon. What's it to you?"

"Not much. But that's not why I'm here. Your name came up in conjunction with Elm Hill, so I'm here to see whether you're willing to help me."

"You're just stupid. You don't even know what's happening."

"Well, what is going on? What do you know about Elm Hill? A sweet innocent nurse has been murdered. I would think that every member of the force would want justice for her."

"What are you saying? That you want me to do your job?"

"No, but I want to know what you know about Elm Hill.

"Why would you think that I would know anything?"

"You had a nice little New Year's party with Victor Buchanan and some gorgeous prostitutes. Now we've got evidence linking Victor to some bad things that are going on at Elm Hill."

"What the hell are you talking about?"

"I can hear some fear in your voice, Twisted. Have you been doing things that will get you sent to the state pen along with Victor? I'm sure you know what they do to cops down there."

"You bastard! Why do you think you can get away with it?"

"You're even stupider than I thought, Twisted. If you get arrested, you'll be on the front page of the *Gazette* for weeks. I'm sure Jimmy Stone can easily find several ladies of the evening to tattle about your perversions and abuse."

"What do you want?"

"I'd guess you're one of the Guardians. How long do you think that you'd last in a jail cell if they thought you might squeal on them? I'd say you can do what I want or end up in Riverview Cemetery."

"Why should I do anything for you? You just said that getting arrested would get me killed, and I doubt that you can protect me as a secret witness. The State's Attorney's office leaks like a sieve."

"Do you think I'm as dumb as you are? I don't want you to testify or even give me a signed statement. We live in a great country. America is large and prosperous. I'm pretty sure that you've got a fair amount of ill-gotten gains salted away somewhere. What I want you to do is tell me what you know informally this morning and then disappear. Go a long way away and start a new life. I'm sure that someone of your talents will soon be doing well."

"Why don't you want me to give testimony or a signed statement? What good will a little chitchat do?"

"It will tell me who to go after about what. Before anybody knows that anything's happening, you should be long gone."

"What do you want to know?"

"Are you a Guardian? Are they up to something with the Griggs gang?"

"You better watch out. We leave the brass alone, and they leave us alone. You go after the Guardians, and you're dead meat. It's a nice thought that I could come back in disguise and spit on your grave. Maybe I'll shit on it, too."

"That's what I like about you Sid. You've always been such a high-class person. I don't care much for either the Guardians or the brass, but I'm smart enough to leave them both alone. What I want to understand, however, is why the Guardians are messing around with Elm Hill."

"Okay, I don't know what good it will do you, but if you want it you can have it. The Guardians have gotten a share of the Griggs gang's profits from gambling, prostitution, and drugs dating back to the 1920s. If you couldn't profit from Prohibition, you were pretty dumb back then, even after the Depression hit. That's why so many of us work vice. You're right. I've got a nice nest egg."

"Thank you, Sid. That's an illuminating piece of background information. But what interest would either the Griggs gang or the Guardians have in a psychiatric hospital for women? That doesn't make sense to me."

"In March, when he was drinking and whoring with us, Victor Buchanan let slip that the Griggs gang was expecting to make big money from something that was going on at Elm Hill. I mentioned it to our captain, and he was suddenly all ears. A few days later, he had us get a sumptuous high-rent hooker for Victor and him. Sometime during the evening, he gave Victor the choice of telling him what he was doing at Elm Hill or having Ed Griggs learn that Victor had loose lips. Victor evidently didn't have to think long before he was willing to cough up what he knew, which wasn't that much. According to him, the Griggs gang was helping some big shots take over the hospital, but he didn't know who they were or what they represented. Their aim was to get enough control of the budget to divert several million dollars a year. Then when the point was reached where the hospital couldn't pay all its bills, they'd use it as an excuse to throw out the honest people in the administration and lay off a significant portion of the staff. This would scare the other employees into silence and allow them to skim off even more money.

"The captain and Victor then talked things over. They decided that Victor would try to sell Ed Griggs on the idea of letting the Guardians participate because having police protection could be valuable. That seemed to work out, so I got the assignment to work with Victor on his end."

"What did you do?"

"What the Griggs gang had sold the guys trying to grab control of Elm Hill was that they could smuggle in contraband that could be planted to create a big scandal. We'd get some people, like that trouble-making bitch of a head nurse, arrested. Then the doc who's in charge of the hospital would have to let our people run things before he gradually got eased out. Our people on the inside were going to plant drugs, guns, and pornography, and a couple of the big shots had enough pull to have the place raided by Vice. Victor was laughing about how they were going to plant lesbo magazines and drugs in the head nurse's office. That way Dora could give her what she deserved. As you know, that plan blew up in our faces. After that, I steered clear of the Elm Hill schemes because too many people were getting wise to what we were doing. The Griggs gang tried again the night that stupid nurse was caught. You must know that the chief is after the jerks in Vice who got caught trying to participate. I guess it's wise to head out before the whole thing explodes."

"Well, Sid, you're certainly not the nicest guy in the world, but you delivered. Good luck wherever you're headed."

Miss Mason seemed excited. "Well done, Richard. Congratulations. I know you can't use any of it for evidence, but at least we know what we're up against and can use the information to protect ourselves if any new scheme arises."

"You can have the tape, Carol. I was planning to give it to you in any event. This is simply too dangerous to have around the police station or even in my house."

Chapter 26 ~ Surprise Attack

About 5:30 that afternoon I got a call from Rachel. She asked me to come down to the Violent Ward to tell my former patients about the major change that had occurred on the ward since I had a rapport with them. When I got there, I noted that about half the patients were out and engaged in normal activities and that none of the staff were wearing protective clothing. Things were obviously getting back to normal. I found Miss Delaware in the lounge listening to the radio, briefly explained what had happened on the ward, and exchanged a few pleasantries before leaving her to her program. Jenny Sachs was in the dayroom, sitting on a bench by the window and confined by a set of iron anklets that were attached to the wall. She saw me coming and smiled almost immediately.

"Hi, Mr. Russell. It's good to see you. As you can see, Miss Weiss has already changed things on the ward and let me come out of my cell without a strait jacket. You can just feel that most of the patients are more relaxed now that tight security isn't being enforced."

"I'm glad you already notice the difference. So much has happened today. Mrs. Greene and Mrs. Wells, the charge nurses for the day night shift, have been arrested for participating in the Nora plot. I think that they wanted to keep the ward tense to keep people from looking too closely at what they had been doing. Miss Rayburn now realizes that her trust in them was really misplaced. When I came down here, Miss Weiss told me that she had appointed Miss Rakowsky as charge nurse for the morning shift."

"That's really great news for me. Thank you for being the bearer of good tidings and for treating me so nicely in the past."

I didn't see Valerie Waller in either the dayroom or the lounge, so I checked her room and found her sitting at the desk and reading. She looked up when I opened the door.

"Why hello, Mr. Russell. It's so good to see you again. After you left the ward, I felt like I didn't have any friends here. But why are you here so late? Don't you usually work on the morning shift?"

"I'm not really working on the Violent Ward anymore. However, Miss Weiss, who just came back on duty, felt that I'd be the best person to tell my former patients about some big events that just happened today."

"Miss Weiss is on duty? Nobody told me. Is she still in trouble with the police? I really liked her. She's so caring."

"The police released her this morning, and she came back on duty as charge nurse for this shift. Mrs. Wells and Mrs. Greene have been arrested. Furthermore, Dr. Rydberg, the hospital Director, reviewed your treatment and interviewed all the people who treated you at the beginning. He clearly thought that something was fishy. He said that he was going to consult Dr. Carson and Dr. Session about you. In all the confusion, I'm not sure if anything's happened there. However, he's suspended your electro-shock until he's received a confirmed diagnosis that would support it."

"That's very nice to hear. Amanda Lowell came to my room yesterday afternoon and gave me an orientation about electro-shock. She scared me, and I'm pretty sure that she enjoyed doing."

"Who's Amanda Lowell? I don't think that I've heard that name before. I thought that Helen Gerlach was Dr. Carson's chief assistant for electro-shock."

"She's a nurse in my dad's clinic back in Springfield. I was shocked when I saw her. She said that Dr. Carson had agreed to teach him how to administer shock therapy and that he had sent her to Elm Hill to learn how to assist in the procedure."

I suddenly had an intuitive leap worthy of Miss Mason. "Is she fairly tall with thick black hair."

"Yes, that's her. Why do you ask?"

"Somebody like that is wanted for questioning. There are two people who've seen her close up. I'll let you know what happens."

When I returned to the clinic, Laura and Emma wanted to check Amanda Lowell out immediately. However, on second thought, Laura decided that she'd wait for the next day and have the police arrange a full identity parade for the suspicious nurse. At 10:45, Laura asked Officer Devlin to go down to the Violent Ward to escort Rachel back to the clinic. I asked if I could go with her, and she said that she'd like the company because I had a key to the ward and because the hospital turned a little spooky at night when the corridors were almost completely deserted. We got there in the middle of the changeover between shifts. Rachel was deep in conversation with the new charge nurse for the night shift, who was evidently concerned about moving to the Violent Ward. When they were done, a worried-looking female attendant approached Rachel quite deferentially.

"Hello, Miss Weiss. I'm Lettie Tuttle. I put Miss Waller into restraints several times under orders from Mrs. Wells. Now, we've heard that Mrs. Wells has been arrested for mistreating Valerie. Please, ma'am. Are you going to have me fired or taken to jail?"

"Of course not, Lettie. You did exactly what you should have by obeying your supervisor. Incidentally, the police arrested Mrs. Wells and Mrs. Greene for crimes that they committed, not because of anything that I said. I'm a nurse, not a policewoman."

The other female attendant spoke up for Lettie.

"She's a really hard worker and pretty diligent about learning how to do the right thing. Mr. Jones has a very high opinion of her."

Rachel smiled at the girl and gave her a reassuring pat on the back.

As we prepared to leave, I suggested that we go up the front stairs rather than the shorter route through a deserted basement since the murderer had yet to be apprehended. When we walked by the front door, we noticed that there wasn't a guard there. This caught Officer Devlin's attention immediately.

"Andy, isn't that door always guarded?"

"Yes. Furthermore, once the evening shift has a chance to leave, it's locked."

We walked over and saw a sign saying, "Mr. Rogers is sick. His replacement will come on duty by 11:30." A quick check of the front door showed that it was unlocked.

Officer Devlin became cautious. "Stay very close together. I don't know whether I should guard your front or your back. Andy, is there anyone else in the hospital besides Laura and me who's armed?

"Not that I know of. I think that Clem may be sleeping somewhere in the administrative suite, but I've never seen him with a gun in Elm Hill. Then again, our guards were never armed until Mary Terwilliger was murdered."

The front staircase up to the second floor was in the middle of the building and was quite wide. The two stairs that went upwards to the third floor had their own stairwells that were out of sight of anyone who was either on the stairs from the second floor or in the main corridor on the third.

I had never paid any attention to this architecture, but now it seemed ominous as it provided a perfect place for an attacker to lurk. Officer Devlin evidently agreed. She told us to walk softly and silently up the stairs. Then, when we reached the stairs to the third floor, she pointed to the left stairwell, drew her automatic, clicked the safety off, and gave us a rueful smile. Nothing happened until we had almost reached the third-floor landing when a woman shrieked from just to our left.

"They're coming up the front!"

A man in a lab coat leaped into view from the stairway at the far end of the hall and extended a handgun in our direction. Since he was half a city block away, aiming wouldn't have done much good.

When she saw our armed attacker, Officer Devlin fired once in his direction and pushed Rachel and me into the alcove in front of the stairs A nurse in full surgical dress was already in it. Seeing just a person's eyes can make them look evil, but this woman was clearly terrified. I had an inspiration.

"Are you Amanda?"

She cried and nodded yes. Officer Devlin sent another round down the hall and then gave her verdict on Amanda.

"Andy, put her hands behind her back and use my cuffs. Rachel, can you find something to gag her?"

I cuffed her far more tightly than I would a patient, and I heard Rachel tearing her uniform to create a gag. As we were doing this, the man fired two more times in our direction, but we were protected in the alcove. Then the hospital's alarm began to blare.

"Rachel. Is there a place we can fortify ourselves on the fourth floor? I'm afraid that he can get too close here and start firing into the alcove before I can get a clear shot at him.

"I know the perfect place. With the alarm, everyplace where there are people will be bolted shut from the inside. Also, the fact that the alarm was set off shows the switchboard is in action. The police should be on their way now."

"Andy and Rachel, get Amanda to the corner of the staircase on the fourth floor. I want to be sure that he's still down here when we make our break, or we might walk into his gun sight."

I was struck by how cool these two young women were in the face of deadly danger. Once we were in position, Officer Devlin stuck just her hand around the corner and fired. When her fire was returned, she motioned us to go and caught up to us by the time we reached the alcove on the fourth floor. She peaked around the corner and then stepped just outside the alcove, taking a position that allowed her to cover both the alcove and the corridor.

"I balanced the doorstop on the door handle, so he'll make a noise if he tries to follow us. Rachel, where are we going?"

"There's a staircase in the middle of the hall that goes up the hospital's tower to the two small rooms that are in it. It's a spiral staircase, so you can set up an ambush almost anyplace along it."

"That sounds good. If the police have already been notified, they should be here within minutes. We shouldn't have to hold him off too long. Listen, Amanda. I don't know what you're doing dressed up like that, but the way that guy is shooting at us indicates that he doesn't seem to take your safety very seriously. You might consider whether he's planning to shoot you and claim that you're the murderess. Now, run along. Andy, wait for me in the first room. I want someone who's familiar with a handgun to be with me in case I get disabled."

We made it to the spiral staircase and had climbed one spiral when we heard a shot followed by a yell from Officer Devlin.

"I'm okay."

Amanda was hurrying as much as she could in her handcuffs and gag, as Officer Devlin had evidently scared her into complete submission. When we got to the room halfway up the tower, Rachel and her prisoner continued upward while I grabbed a heavy table and dragged it to the door. Officer Devlin appeared a minute or two later, and we turned the table on its side and shoved it up under the door handle.

"That's good thinking, Andy. The door opens inward. He'll really have to shove it to get in here. Now let's push that couch over to the corner giving us a direct sight on where he'll come in. Good. Crouch in the corner, and I'll squeeze in next to you. Okay, you're next to my right hand so that if I'm hit you can grab my weapon."

We waited in silence and soon heard heavy footsteps coming up the stairs. He stopped, pushed at the door, and then called in a normal tone of voice, "Amanda, I'll save you. Just tell me if you're in there."

Suddenly, he threw himself violently against the door and then staggered through the opening as table fell and the door swung inwards.

Officer Devlin fired twice. The man screamed, dropped his gun, disappeared through the door as the force of the bullets drove him sideways and backwards. He bumped down the steps for what seemed like a very long time.

Officer Devlin was rigid, and I thought she might be in shock. I took the gun from her and got her settled on the couch.

"Oh, Andy. I've killed him! It's so horrible. I've never hurt anyone before. I feel so guilty."

I put my arms around her, and she burrowed her small body into mine, crying softly.

"Don't feel like that. You were so brave. You saved all our lives. You're such a good person."

I had called up to Rachel that the crisis had ended. She brought Amanda down, and the four of us sat together in silence until Detective Perkins came.

"I apologize for what all of you had to go through. I know you've been traumatized. You should all talk to Dr. Harvey and Emma tomorrow. On a lighter note, Miss Mason was the city's best detective again. Dr. Sessions was the killer."

"How did she know that?"

"Well, that's a little embarrassing. While most of us were sniggering at the image of a transvestite doctor enjoying a hooded prostitute, she was the only one who realized that there's not a girdle in the world that could hide Dr. Carson's paunch. Consequently, Doctor Sessions was left as the prime suspect."

Chapter 27 ~ New Beginnings

In all, five police officers and four members of the Griggs gang where arrested in the investigation of criminal activity and corruption involving Elm Hill. Nobody was charged in the murder of Mary Terwilliger since it was assumed to have been a wanton act by the vicious doctor that neither the Griggs gang nor the Guardians would have countenanced. Unlike the aftermath of the Adams murder, the movers and shakers of Osloville moved decisively to ensure that Elm Hill would be protected from any new attacks. The defendants kept their mouths shut and marched off to prison like good soldiers. The Guardians and the Griggs gang still controlled the city's underworld, but took a much lower profile and, at least as far as the *Gazette* was concerned, left honest folks alone.

No businessman, not even Bernard Ernst or Mark Reynolds, was ever mentioned publicly in connection with the case. However, their influence over Elm Hill was quickly ended. Ernst resigned from the Board, citing increased business responsibility. Reynolds, for his part, made the headlines for receiving a huge state contract for work in State Capital and moved the headquarters of Reynolds Construction and his personal residence there. The Elm Hill Board changed significantly as there were four resignations. Three prominent businessmen with sterling reputations and a college President were added to the Board. The positions of Dr. Rydberg and Miss Mason became unassailable. Several, including Dr. Rydberg and Miss Mason, were suspicious of Miss Rayburn and especially of Dr. Carson. However, no concrete evidence against them turned up, so they kept their positions. Miss Rayburn announced that she'd retire in two years when she turned sixty and move to Minneapolis where she had family. Dr. Rydberg announced that Rachel would replace her as nurse nanager. Much to my surprise, Miss Rayburn embraced her and praised her professional accomplishments at a meeting with the whole Violent Ward staff.

Officer Devlin, of course, was a heroine who received star treatment from the *Osloville Gazette*. This evidently created something of a problem for the police department because there was no career ladder for policewomen and she was too young and new to the force to even be considered for a promotion. Also, remembering how tightly she had pressed her tortured body into mine, I wondered whether she wanted to continue a career that might involve violence. Police Chief Richardson solved the problem nicely by making her the department's liaison officer for dealing with the press and the community. Pictures of her attractive face replaced stories about corruption in the *Gazette*'s coverage of the police.

I also finally learned about how Rachel's heart-rending note had been sent to me. Two days after the death of Dr. Sessions, Emma came into my room in the clinic to wake me, closing the heavy metal door behind her.

"Hi, Andy. I wanted to tell you something where nobody can overhear us. I was the one who sent you the letter from Rachel. It came to Brackman in an envelope that was postmarked Osloville and had a return address on Forsyth Lane. I looked at the map of the city and couldn't find any Forsyth Lane."

"Did you tell Miss Mason about it?"

"No, but she asked me whether I had sent it to you after you showed it to her. That's why I was watching what you packed in your room before moving over here. She made it clear that the policewomen couldn't be permitted to see it."

When I asked Miss Mason later that day why she thought Emma had been involved with the letter, she smiled.

"I talked about Emma with the cute little matron at the jail while she was helping transport Carrie Adams to Elm Hill. That was about the only possible connection between someone at the jail and someone here that I could think of. Why don't we go to church this Sunday and see if she'll chat with us?"

"Do you go to Trinity Lutheran?"

"I think that we're both a little irregular in our attendance, so this Sunday should be a good time to catch up."

We waited for Emily outside the choir's dressing room after the service. She seemed excited when Miss Mason invited her to chat in a small office over coffee and sweet rolls. She detoured to tell her parents that somebody else would bring her home.

"Hi, Emily. It's great to see you. You know Andy Russell who came to Elm Hill from State University as a summer assistant for me."

We sat down, filled our coffee cups, and passed the plate of sweet buns around. Miss Mason smiled, said that we were being good Lutherans, and asked Emily if she had sent a letter to Emma Hughes.

The girl looked a little embarrassed and nodded.

"I asked Rachel if she knew someone named Emma who had been hassled by the police. She said yes and suggested I send the letter to her at Brackman Hall. You scared me a little with how great a detective you are."

"There's no need for you to be frightened. We've got lots of catching up to do. When we met in April, you were a timid meter maid who had lost her boyfriend. Now, you have a shiny diamond on your finger and are a tough-looking jail matron.

"Oh, ma'am. You're right. Two wonderful things have happened. I took your advice and went to see Bob at work at his dad's auto repair shop. A storm provided a good excuse to ask him to give me a ride home and meant that my uniform was covered up with my raincoat. Andy, that may sound crazy to you, but he broke up with me in January, saying that my uniform made me look too domineering for him.

"He seemed glad to see me, although the three other mechanics snickered and made some low comments that I'm awfully glad I couldn't hear. He gave them a dirty look and went to ask his dad for permission to run me home since it was about closing time. His dad smiled at me and told us to enjoy ourselves. When we got to his car, I asked if he liked me better with my uniform covered up. He looked very sheepish and apologized to me for being so mean. He said the other mechanics had been mocking him and saying that he wanted to be handcuffed to a policewoman. He soon realized that they were just jealous because he'd inherit the business one day and had such a pretty girlfriend. I started to cry, and he asked if I forgave him. When I nodded, he gave me the longest and hardest kiss he ever had. When we got to my house, he waited for my dad to come home asked if he had any objections to his proposing marriage to me. My dad and mom were shocked and so happy for me. Even my sister Sally gave me a hug. Oh, ma'am. Thanks to you, I'm engaged."

Emily was definitely a radiant fiancée. She then hurried on to her second piece of good news.

"In early June, my supervisor ordered me to report to her office in the central police station at two that afternoon. When I got there, I was met by jail Matron Marian Rawlings who works the 3-to-11 shift. She's the nicest of the Matrons. She said that because the number of women prisoners has increased considerably since the War, the matrons on the day and evening shifts were being given an aide to help control them. She said that she picked me because I'm good with people, but I really wonder if it's connected to the Adams murder."

Nurse Mason smiled slightly but still looked serious. "You're probably right. In any case, Emily, you're starting to think like a detective. What else did she say?"

"She said that I'd get a major pay increase and would start on the next Monday. She asked if I had any questions. I told her I'd love to work for her, but I had some worries about my qualifications. I'd never even held a gun, didn't know how to use handcuffs, and might be afraid to administer a strip search. She laughed and said there shouldn't be any problems. She pulled a set of handcuffs from her belt and showed me how to put them on, snug without being too tight, and how to unlock them. Since she had about half a dozen on her belt, she gave me the cuffs and the keys and suggested that I practice on my sister at home. Then she said that the male jailers didn't let the matrons carry weapons because they were afraid that prisoners could take them away from us, so the matrons have wooden nightsticks which are more than enough to control their prisoners. Finally, she promised that she'd teach me about strip searching but that, unlike the handcuffs and leg chains that I'd have to use right away, this could be done gradually. She made it sound easy, so I accepted right away. Also, she's nice. I don't think that I could work for someone who's mean like Matron Butler. That night when I started to practice handcuffing on her, Sally tried to resist, but mom made her do it. Once I got good at it, I left her in them for fifteen minutes as we watched TV. Then she came over, kissed me on the cheek, and said that I was a real policewoman."

I went back to State U. in mid-September. It was great to get back to my academic home and away from the dangers at Elm Hill. For my fall semester, I was to take three classes and do some data gathering for Dr. Calder's research project. Then in the Spring, I wouldn't take any classes to free me for travel to psychiatric hospitals around the Midwest to do interviewing and observation with Linda Sherry and Bill Watkins. Surprisingly perhaps, neither Linda nor Bill seemed jealous that I had been named the head graduate student on the research project. Linda was newly married and glad to avoid more duties. Bill said that he was very interested in the subject matter but not in the administrative work of keeping our project in good running order. We got on very well.

I was sitting by myself in our research office at the beginning of our third week of classes when there was a knock. When I opened the door, a beautiful girl with reddish hair walked in and sat in our visitors' chair. Her face was shaded by a large hat that she wore at an angle.

"Hello, Mr. Russell. I'm Julie Benton. I'm a freshman psychology major. I really like the Intro to Psych class that I'm taking now."

"Hi. I think that you've come to the wrong person. Mr. Scott is the teaching assistant for that class. His office is on the second floor."

"No, it's you I'm looking for. I have a couple of questions for you."

"Well, I'd certainly be glad to help if I can, but it's been four years since I took the class. I'm just a research assistant now."

"That sounds interesting. What are you working on?"

"It's Dr. Calder's big research project on psychiatric hospitals. Who are you, anway?"

"I'm just starting my college classes, of course. Also, I'm a Pi Phi pledge, by the way."

I laughed, perhaps with a little disappointment. "I see now. My sister Jennifer got you to tease me."

"Obviously, I know Jennifer, but why do you think I'm teasing you?"

"You're a beautiful girl. I guess that Jennifer thought that I might try to pick you up and then get really disappointed."

"I don't think that she's mean like that. Anyway, you've just answered the first of my four possible questions affirmatively, so are you ready for question two? Also, I should say thank you for your compliment. I wasn't fishing for one."

"Well, Miss Benton, you speak in riddles, but this is certainly more pleasant than thinking about electro-shock therapy."

"I'm not a fan of electro-shocks either. They're really frightening, but let's move on to number two. In a couple of weeks, we're having a

Halloween dance. I'm trying to see whether I should be forward and invite you. You've just indicated that you're available. Can you dance?"

"Yes, although Jennifer would tell you with some justification that I'm a little clumsy."

"We can always practice."

"Why would you ask me? Somehow, I don't see myself as a dream vision for a sorority girl."

"If we get to question four, it should be clear. So, let's go to number three. Would you demand that a date go to bed with you?"

"No, I really believe that that represents a serious commitment that should not be taken very lightly."

"Well, just one more, but this could unnerve you. Did Nurse Mason take you to bed?"

My jaw literally dropped open. "How do you know about her? What did Jennifer say about her? Why would you want to know something like that?"

"She's so strong that I couldn't compete with her memory."

"You're right about that. I couldn't conceive that she'd be interested in making love to me, however. But, how are you connected with her?"

She took off her hat, fluffed out her hair, and smiled most attractively.

"You don't recognize me, do you?"

"No, somehow I'm sure that I'd remember if I'd seen you."

"Well, I remember how nice you were to me when I was facing electro-shock, and my friend Mrs. Ward really thought that you treated her very well. Don't look so lost. I guess you've never seen me when my hair was nice. I'm Carrie, Judge Adams' daughter."

About the Author

Cal is an Emeritus Professor of Political Science at Auburn University. *A Strait Jacket for Sarah* is the sequel to *The Black Angels* (ATTMP. 2015). In addition, he has authored or edited 26 academic books. He grew up in New Jersey where he graduated from St. Bernard's School and then received a B.A. from Beloit College and a Ph.D. in Political Science from the University of Illinois, in the Midwest where the mysteries are set. He taught at New Mexico State University in the 1970s and the University of Wyoming in the 1980s before moving to Auburn in 1992. He served as President of the American Association for Chinese Studies (2002-2004) and won the Auburn Alumni Association's Award for Minority Advancement (2007), the College of Liberal Arts' Excellence in Advising Award (2004), and the Student Government Association's Outstanding Graduate Faculty Member Award (2012), as well as receiving a Pi Sigma Alpha Award for Teaching Excellence from the American Political Science Association (1998). He and Janet, his wife of 50 years who is also a retired Political Science Professor, reside in Auburn. They have three daughters, who are very excited about the publication of this novel, and they enjoy reading, hiking, and going to the theatre.

FOR MORE INFORMATION ON TITLES AVAILABLE FROM

ALL THINGS THAT MATTER PRESS, GO TO

http://allthingsthatmatterpress.com

or contact us at

allthingsthatmatterpress@gmail.com

If you enjoyed this book, please post a review on Amazon.com

and your favorite social media sites.

Thank you!